T4-AIK-306

816.4
Loc

97476

Locke.
Swinging round the
cirkle.

Date Due

The Library
Nazareth College of Rochester, N. Y.

PRINTED
in U.S.A.

SWINGIN

ROUND THE CIRKLE

by

David R. Locke

LITERATURE HOUSE / GREGG PRESS

Upper Saddle River, N. J.

NAZARETH COLLEGE LIBRARY

Republished in 1969 by

LITERATURE HOUSE

an imprint of The Gregg Press

121 Pleasant Avenue

Upper Saddle River, N. J. 07458

97476

Standard Book Number—8398-1167-5

Library of Congress Card—72-91085

Printed in United States of America

816.4
Loc

THE AMERICAN HUMORISTS

Art Buchwald, Bob Hope, Red Skelton, S. J. Perelman, and their like may serve as reminders that the "cheerful irreverence" which W. D. Howells, two generations ago, noted as a dominant characteristic of the American people has not been smothered in the passage of time. In 1960 a prominent Russian literary journal called our comic books "an infectious disease." Both in Russia and at home, Mark Twain is still the best-loved American writer; and Mickey Mouse continues to be adored in areas as remote as the hinterland of Taiwan. But there was a time when the mirthmakers of the United States were a more important element in the gross national product of entertainment than they are today. In 1888, the British critic Grant Allen gravely informed the readers of the *Fortnightly*: "Embryo Mark Twains grow in Illinois on every bush, and the raw material of *Innocents Abroad* resounds nightly, like the voice of the derringer, through every saloon in Iowa and Montana." And a half-century earlier the English reviewers of our books of humor had confidently asserted them to be "the one distinctly original product of the American mind"–"an indigenous home growth." Scholars are today in agreement that humor was one of the first vital forces in making American literature an original entity rather than a colonial adjunct of European culture.

The American Humorists Series represents an effort to display both the intrinsic qualities of the national heritage of native prose humor and the course of its development. The books are facsimile reproductions of original editions hard to come by—some of them expensive collector's items. The series includes examples of the early infiltration of the autochthonous into the stream of jocosity and satire inherited from Europe but concentrates on representative products of the outstanding practitioners. Of these the earliest in point of time are the exemplars of the Yankee "Down East" school, which began to flourish in the 1830's— and, later, provided the cartoonist Thomas Nast with the idea for Uncle Sam, the national personality in striped pants. The series follows with the chief humorists who first used the Old Southwest as setting. They were the founders of the so-called frontier humor.

The remarkable burgeoning of the genre during the Civil War period is well illustrated in the books by David R. Locke, "Bill Arp," and others who accompanied Mark Twain on the way to fame in the jesters' bandwagon. There is a volume devoted to Abraham Lincoln as jokesmith and spinner of tall tales. The wits and satirists of the Gilded Age, the Gay Nineties, and the first years of the present century round out the sequence. Included also are several works which mark the rise of Negro humor, the sort that made the minstrel show the first original contribution of the United States to the world's show business.

The value of the series to library collections in the field of American literature is obvious. And since the subjects treated in these books, often with surprising realism, are intimately involved with the political and social scene, and the Civil War, and above all possess sectional characteristics, the series is also of immense value to the historian. Moreover, quite a few of the volumes carry illustrations by the ablest cartoonists of their day, a matter of interest to the student of the graphic arts. And, finally, it should not be overlooked that the specimens of Negro humor offer more tangible evidence of the fixed stereotyping of the Afro-American mentality than do the slave narratives or the abolitionist and sociological treatises.

The American Humorists Series shows clearly that a hundred years ago the jesters had pretty well settled upon the topics that their countrymen were going to laugh at in the future—from the Washington merry-go-round to the pranks of local hillbillies. And as for the tactics of provoking the laugh, these old masters long since have demonstrated the art of titillating the risibilities. There is at times mirth of the highbrow variety in their pages: neat repartee, literary parody, Attic salt, and devastating irony. High seriousness of purpose often underlies their fun, for many of them wrote with the conviction that a column of humor was more effective than a page of editorials in bringing about reform or combating entrenched prejudices. All of the time-honored devices of the lowbrow comedians also abound: not only the sober-faced exaggeration of the tall tale, outrageous punning, and grotesque spelling, but a boisterous Homeric joy in the rough-and-tumble. There may be more beneath the surface, however, for as one of their number, J. K. Bangs, once remarked, these old humorists developed "the exuberance of feeling and a resentment of restraint that have helped to make us the free and independent people that we are." The native humor is indubitably American, for it is infused with the customs, associations, convictions, and tastes of the American people.

PROFESSOR CLARENCE GOHDES
Duke University
January, 1969   *Durham, North Carolina*

DAVID ROSS LOCKE

David Ross Locke was born in Vestal, New York, in 1833, the son of Nathaniel Reed Locke, a Revolutionary War soldier, and Hester (Ross) Locke. At the age of ten, he was apprenticed as a printer's devil to the Cortland, New York, *Democrat,* where he remained until 1850. His apprenticeship finished, he worked as an itinerant printer, travelling in both the North and the South. It was during these years that he encountered and learned to detest the white trash whom he was to satirize ten years later in the "Nasby Letters." In 1852 he founded the Plymouth, Ohio, *Advertiser,* and married Martha Bodine. In 1856 he started the Bucyrus, Ohio, *Journal,* to which he contributed short stories. Two meetings with Abraham Lincoln in 1858 and 1859, and the beginning of the Secessionist movement projected the young radical newspaperman into a career of political journalism which was to make him the most famous pro-Northern propagandist of the Civil War and Reconstruction Eras. In 1861 Locke assumed the editorship of the Findlay, Ohio, *Jeffersonian,* and it was in this paper that the first "Nasby Letter" appeared. The letters were collected and published as a book in 1864. In 1865, Locke visited Lincoln in Washington, and then went to Toledo, Ohio, to become Editor of the *Blade,* which he later bought. He was Editor, for a short time, of the New York *Evening Mail.* Although offered political posts by both Lincoln and Grant, Locke's only political ambition was to become an alderman of the Third Ward of Toledo, a goal which he attained in 1886. He died of tuberculosis two years later.

Locke was a prolific writer. Not only did he publish newspaper articles and the immortal "Nasby Letters," but he wrote political pamphlets, essays, a narrative poem, and two very good novels. The "Nasby Letters" made him wealthy and famous, and are in print today in several editions.

"Petroleum Vesuvius Nasby, late pastor uv the Church of the New Dispensation, Chaplain to his Excellency the President, and p. m. at Confederate x roads, Kentucky," epitomized Locke's hatred of the ignorant, bigoted, anti-democratic, cowardly Southerners—the "Copperheads," who ranted about the necessity for Negro slavery and backed up their arguments with quotations torn from the Old Testament. These Letters were admired by his friend Lincoln, who said, a month before his assassination, "For the genius to write these things, I would gladly give up my office." And Grant called Locke "the fourth arm of the service" in the Civil War. The Letters were an immediate success with the Northern public, especially after the great political cartoonist Thomas Nast began to illustrate them.

In the "Nasby Letters," Locke utilized humorous devices such as misspellings, deformed grammar, *non sequiturs,* hyperbole, and fantastic juxtaposition of ideas, in order to caricature the warped intellectual processes of the country parson who "wrote" them. In his novels, which are equally bitter in their contempt for the baser elements of society, Locke adopts a more conventional, narrative literary style, that of the omniscient author. And his target is economic greed and mismanagement instead of ignorance and racism.

Swingin' Round the Cirkle (1867) contains forty-one of the best of the "Nasby Letters," as well as a "Prefis." The collection is dedicated to President Johnson (the first), who "might hev bin Diktater." The book contains some of Nasby's particularly fulsome remarks concerning the newly emancipated slaves: "[they] hev bin in bondage so long that they're used to it." He recommends that the Southerners "tear down the nigger school houses and churches wich hev bin built here and there, and kindly take the nigger by the ear, and lead him back to his old quarters." The sarcastic caricatures of Southerners in this work are disagreeable reading, but then nobody has ever accused Locke of writing the "Nasby Letters" for the amusement of the public; of "speaking the truth laughing."

The Morals of Abou Ben Adhem (1875), which the author describes as "Eastern fruit on Western dishes," displays his remarkable versatility as a lowbrow humorist. It is free from the phonetic spellings of the "Nasby Letters." Adhem, a counterfeiter and charlatan from Maine, comes to New Jersey, where he serves up the wisdom of Persia and Egypt to simple folk in need of advice.

Upper Saddle River, N. J.   F. C. S.
May, 1969

NASBY'S DREAM OF PERFECT BLISS.   Page 194.

"Swingin Round the Cirkle."

BY

PETROLEUM V. NASBY,

LATE PASTOR OF THE CHURCH OF THE NEW DISPENSATION,
CHAPLAIN TO HIS EXCELLENCY THE PRESIDENT, AND
P. M. AT CONFEDERATE X ROADS, KENTUCKY.

HIS IDEAS OF

MEN, POLITICS, AND THINGS,

AS SET FORTH IN HIS LETTERS TO THE PUBLIC
PRESS, DURING THE YEAR 1866.

Illustrated by Thomas Nast.

BOSTON:
LEE AND SHEPARD.
1867.

Entered, according to Act of Congress, in the year 1866, by

LEE AND SHEPARD,

In the Clerk's Office of the District Court of the District of Massachusetts.

STEREOTYPED AT THE
BOSTON STEREOTYPE FOUNDRY,
4 Spring Lane.

DEDIKASHUN UV THIS BOOK.

TO

ANDROO JOHNSON,

THE PRIDE AND HOPE UV DIMOCRISY,

Who hez bin Alderman uv his native village,
Guvner uv his State,
Member uv the lower house uv Congress,
And likewise uv the Senit,
Vice President and President, and might hev bin Diktater,
But who is, nevertheless, a Humble Individooal;
Who hez swung around the entire cirkle uv offishl
honor, without feelin his Oats much;
The first public man who considered my
services worth payin for;

AND TO

A L E X.   W.   R A N D A L L ,
POSTMASTER GENRAL,
His most devoted Servant,
Whose autograph adorns my Commishn ez Postmaster,

This Volume

IS RESPECTFULLY DEDIKATED.

CONTENTS.

PREFIS,

OR

INTERDUCTRY CHAPTER.

THERE is a vacancy in the mind uv the public for jist sich a book ez this, else it had never bin published. There is a vacancy in my pockit for the money I am to reseeve ez copy-rite, else I hed never slung together, in consecootive shape, the ijees wich I hev from time to time flung out thro the public press, for the enlitenment uv an ongrateful public and the guidance uv an obtoose Dimocracy.

I didn't put these thots uv mine upon paper for amoozement. There hezn't bin anythin amoozin in Dimocrisy for the past five years, and the standard-bearers, the captins uv fifties and hundreds, the leaders uv the hosts, hev hed a ruther rough time uv it. Our prominence made us uncomfortable, for we hev bin the mark uv every writer, every orator, ez

(7)

well ez uv every egg-thrower, in the country. When
that gileless patriot, Jeems Bookannon, retired to private life, regretted by all who held office under him,
Dimocracy felt that she wuz entrin upon a period uv
darknis and gloom. The effort our Suthern brethrin
made for their rites, rendered the position uv us
Northern Dimocrats eggstremely precarious. We
coodent go back on our friends South, for, knowin
that peace must come, and that when it did come we
wood hev to, ez in the olden time, look to them for
support and maintenance, it behooved us to keep on
their good side. This wood hev bin easy enuff, but
alars! there are laws agin treason, and two-thirds
uv the misguided people north hed got into a way
uv thinkin that the Dimocrasy South had committed
that crime, and they intimated that ef we overstepped
the line that divides loyalty from treason by so much
ez the millionth part uv a hair, they'd make us suffer
the penalty they hoped to mete out to them, but
wich, owin to Johnson, they dident, and wat's more,
can't. Halleloogy!

But I anticipate. Twict I wuz drafted into a service I detested — twict I wuz torn from the buzzum
uv my family, wich I wuz gittin along well enough,
even ef the wife uv my buzzum wood occasionally
git obstinit, and refooze to give me sich washin

money ez wuz nessary to my existence, preferrin to squander it upon bread and clothes for the children, — twict, I say, I wuz pulled into the servis, and twict I wuz forced to desert to the Dimocrisy uv the south, rather than fite agin em. When finally the thumb uv my left hand wuz acksidentally shot off, owin to my foot becomin entangled into the lock uv my gun, wich thumb wuz also accidentally across the muzzle thereof, and I wuz no longer liable to military dooty and cood bid Provost Marshels defiance, I only steered clear uv Scylla to go bumpin onto Charybdis. I coodent let Dimocrisy alone, and the eggins — the ridin upon rails — the takin uv the oath — but why shood I harrow up the public buzzum? I stood it all till one nite I wuz pulled out uv bed, compelled to kneel onto my bare knees in the cold snow, the extremity uv my under garment, wich modesty forbids me to menshun the name uv it, fluttrin in a Janooary wind, and by a crowd uv laffin soljers compelled to take the oath and drink a pint uv raw, undilooted water! That feather broke the back uv the camel. The oath give me inflamashen uv the brane and the water inflamashen uv the stumick, and for six long weeks I lay, a wreck uv my former self. Ez I arose from that bed and saw in a glass the remains uv my pensive beauty, I vowed to wage a unceasin war on the party wich caused sich havoc, and I hev kept my oath.

I hev bin in the Apossel biznis more extensively than any man sence the time uv Paul. First I established a church uv Democrats in a little oasis I diskivered in the ablishn state uv Ohio, to wit, at Wingert's Corners, where ther wuz four groceries, but nary church or skool-house within four miles, and whose populashen wuz unanimously Dimocratic, the grocery keepers hevin mortgages on all the land around em — but alars! I wuz forced to leeve it after the election of Linkin in 1864. Noo Gersey bein the only state North wich wuz onsquelched, to her I fled, and at Saint's Rest (wich is in Noo Gersey) I erected another tabernacle. There I stayed, and et and drank and wuz merry, but Ablishnism pursood me thither, and in the fall uv '65 that state got ornery and cussid, and went Ablishn, and agin, like the wandrin Jew, I wuz forced to pull up, and wend my weary way to Kentucky, where, at Confedrit ✕ Roads, I feel that I am safe. Massychoosets ideas can't penetrate us here. The aristocracy bleeve in freedom uv speech, but they desire to exercise a supervision over it, that they may not be led astray. They bleeve they 'r rite, and for fear they'd be forced to change their

minds, whenever they git into argument with anybody, ef the individooal gits the better uv them, they
to-wunst shoot him ez a disturber. Hence Massychoosits can't disturb us here; the populashen is
unanimously Democratic, and bids fair to continyoo so.

Here I hope to spend the few remainin years uv a
eventful life. Here in the enjoyment uv that end uv
the hopes uv all Democrats, a Post Offis, with four
well-regulated groceries within a stun's throw, and
a distillery ornamentin the landscape only a quarter
uv a mile from where I rite these lines, with the
ruins uv a burnt nigger school house within site uv
my winder, from wich rises the odor, grateful to a
Democratic nostril, and wich he kin snuff afar off,
and say ha! ha! to, uv a half dozen niggers wich
wuz consumed when it wuz burned, wat more kin I
want? I feel that I am more than repaid for all my
suffrins, and that I shel sale smoothly down the
stream uv time, unvexed and happy.

It is proper to state that the papers uv which this
volume is composed wuz written at various times
and under various circumstances. They reflect the
mind uv the author doorin a most eventful year in
his history, and mark the condition uv the Dimocrisy
from week to week. Consekently they shift from

grave to gay, from lively to severe, with much alacrity, the grate party seemin at times to be lifted onto
the top wave uv success, and at other times bein
down in the trough uv despondency and despair.

I mite say more, but wherefore? Ez the record
uv a year uv hopes and fears, uv exaltation and
depression, it may possess interest or may not —
'cordin to the style uv the reader. Whatever may
be its fate, one thing I am certin uv, to wit: I am a
reglerly commissioned P. M.; and while the ap-
proval of the public mite lighten the toils uv offishl
life and sweeten the whisky wich the salary
purchases, the frowns uv the said public can't redoose me to the walks uv private life. They can't
frown me out uv offis, nor frown P. M. General
Randall's name off my commishn.

P. V. N.

POST OFFIS, CONFEDRIT X ROADS
   (wich is in the State uv Kentucky), Oct. 1, 1866.

SWINGIN ROUND THE CIRKLE.

I.

After the New Jersey Election, 1865.

Saint's Rest
(wich is in the State uv Noo Gersey),
November, 9, 1865.

NEVER wuz I in so pleasant a frame uv mind as last night. All wuz peace with me, for after bein buffeted about the world for three skore years, at last it seemed to me ez tho forchune, tired uv persekootin a unforchnit bein, hed taken me into favor. I hed a solemn promise from the Demekratic State Central Committy in the great State uv Noo Gersey, that ez soon ez our candidate for Governor wuz dooly elected, I shood hev the position uv Dorekeeper to the House uv the Lord (wich in this State means the Capital, & wich is certainly better than dwellin in the tents uv wicked grosery keepers, on tick, ez I do), and a joodishus exhibition uv this

(13)

promise hed prokoored for me unlimited facilities
for borrerin, wich I improved, muchly.

On Wednesday nite I wuz a sittin in my room, a
enjoyin the pleasin reflection that in a few days I
should be placed above want & beyond the contin-
gencies uv fortune. Wood! oh wood! that I hed
died then and there, before that dream ov bliss wuz
roodly broken. A wicked boy cum runnin past
with a paper wich he hed brot from the next town
where there lives a man who takes one. He flung
it thro the window to me and past on. I opened it
eagerly, and glanced at the hed lines!

"NOO GERSEY — 5,000 REPUBLIKIN!"

One long and piercin shreek wuz heard thro that
house, and wen the inmates rushed into the room
they found me inanymate on the floor. The fatal
paper lay near me, explainin the cause uv the catas-
trophe. The kind-hearted landlord, after feelin uv
my pockets and diskiverin that the contents thereof
wood not pay the arrearages uv board, held a hur-
ried consultation with his wife as to the propriety
uv bringin me to; he insisting that it wuz the only
chance uv gittin what wuz back — she insistin that
ef I was brung to I'd go on runnin up the bill, bigger and bigger, and never pay at last. While they

was argooin the matter, pro and con, I happened to git a good smell uv his breath, wich restored me to consciousniss to-wunst, without further assistance.

When in trouble my poetic sole alluz finds vent in song. Did ever poet who delited in tombs, and dark, rollin streams, and consumption, and blighted hopes, and decay, and sich themes, ever hev such a pick of subjects ez I hev at this time? The follerin may be a consolation to the few Dimokrats uv the North who have gone so far into copperheadism that they can't change their base: —

A WALE!

In the mornin we go forth rejoicin in our strength — in the evenin we are bustid and wilt!

Man born uv woman (and most men are) is uv few days, & them is so full uv trouble that it's skarsely worth while bein born at all.

In October I waded in woe knee-deep, and now the waters uv afflickshun are about my chin.

I look to the east, and Massychusets rolls in Ablishun.

To the west I turn my eyes, and Wisconsin, and Minnesota, and Illinoy ansers Ablishun.

Southward I turn my implorin gaze, and Maryland sends greetin — Ablishun.

In New York we had em, for lo! we run a soljer, who fought valiantly, and we put him on a platform, wich stunk with nigger — yea, the savor thereof wuz louder than the Ablishun platform itself.

But behold! the people jeer and flout, and say "the platform stinketh loud enough, but the smell thereof is *not* the smell uv the Afrikin — it is of the rotten material uv wich it is composed, and the corrupshun they hev placed upon it" — and New York goes Ablishun.

Slocum held hisself up, and sed, "Come and buy." And our folks bought him and his tribe, but he getteth not his price.

NOO GERSEY — ABLISHUN!!

Job's cattle wuz slain by murrain and holler horn and sich, and, not livin near Noo York, the flesh thereof he cood not sell.

But Job hed suthin left — still cood he sell the hides and tallow!

Lazarus hed sores, but he hed dorgs to lick them.

Noo Gersey wuz the hide & tallow uv the Dimocrisy, and lo! that is gone.

What little is left uv the Dimocrisy is all sore, but where is the dorg so low as to lick it!

Noo Gersey wuz our ewe lamb — lo! the strong hand uv Ablishnism hez taken it.

Noo Gersey wuz the Aryrat on wich our ark rested — behold! the dark waves uv Ablishnism sweep over it!

Darkness falls over me like a pall — the shadder uv woe encompasseth me.

Down my furrowed cheeks rolleth the tears uv anguish, varyin in size from a large Pea to a small tater.

Noo Gersey will vote for the Constooshnel Amendment, and lo! the Nigger will possess the land.

I see horrid visions!

On the Camden and Amboy, nigger brakesmen; and at the polls, niggers!

Where shall we find refuge?

In the North? Lo! it is barred agin us by Ablishnism.

In the South? In their eyes the Northern copperhead findeth no favor.

In Mexico? There is war there, and we might be drafted.

Who will deliver us? Who will pluck us from the pit into wich we hev fallen?

Where I shel go the Lord only knows, but my impression is, South Karliny will be my future home. Wade Hampton is electid Governor, certin, and in that noble State, one may perhaps preserve enough uv the old Dimokratic States Rites to leaven the whole lump.

"I'm aflote — I'm aflote
On the dark rollin sea."

And into what harbor fate will drive my weather-beaten bark, the undersigned can not trooly say.

Noo Gersey — farewell! The world may stand it a year or two, but I doubt it.

Mournfly and sadly,

PETROLEUM V. NASBY,
Lait Paster uv the Church uv the Noo Dispensashun.

II.

A Conversation with General McStinger, of the State of Georgia, which is interrupted by a Subjugated Rebel.

WASHINGTON, D. C., Nov. 18, 1865.

SENCE the November elections I hev bin spendin' the heft uv my time in Washinton. I find a melankoly pleasure in ling'rin around the scene uv so many Demokratic triumphs. Here it wuz that Brooks, the heroic, bludgeoned Sumner; here it wuz that Calhoon, & Yancey, and Breckinridge achieved their glory and renown. Besides, it's the easiest place to dodge a board bill in the Yoonited States. There's so many Congressmen here who resemble me, that I hev no difficulty in passin for one, two-thirds uv the time.

Yesterday I met, in the readin-room uv Willard's, Ginral MacStinger, of South Karliny. The Ginral is here on the same bizness most uv the Southern men hev in this classic city, that uv prokoorin a pardon, wich he hed prokoored, and wuz gittin ready to go home and accept the nominashen for Congress in his deestrick.

The Ginral wuz gloomy. Things didn't soot him, he observed, and he wuz afeerd that the country wuz on the high road to rooin. He hed bin absent from the Yoonited States suthin over four yeers, wich time he hed spent in the southern confederacy. When he went out the Constooshnel Dimocrisy hed some rites wich wuz respected. On his return wat did he see? The power in the hands uv Radikals, Ablishnism in the majority everywhere, a ex-tailor President, — a state uv affairs disgustin in the extreme to the highly sensitive Southern mind. He had accepted a pardon only becoz he felt hisself constrained to put hisself in2 position to go to Congress, that the country might be reskood from its impendin peril. He shood go to Congress, and then he should ask the despots who now hev control, whether, —

1. They spozed the South wood submit to hoomiliatin condishns?

2. What Androo Johnson means by dictatin to the Convenshuns uv sovereign States?

"Why," sez he, "but a few days ago this boor hed the ashoorence to write to the Georgy Convenshun that it ' *must not* ' — mark the term — ' MUST not assoom the confedrit war debt.' Is a tailor to say ' *must not* ' to shivelrus Georgy? Good God! — where are we driftin? For one, I never will be consilliated on them terms — never! I never wuz used to that style uv talk in Dimekratic conven- shuns.

"Ez soon ez I take my seet in Congris," resoomed he, " I shel deliver a speech, wich I writ the day after Lee surrendered, so ez to hev it ready, in which I shel take the follerin ground, to wit:

" That the South hev buried the hatchit, and hev diskivered that they love the old Yoonion above eny thing on earth. But,

" The North must meet us half way, or we wont be answerable for the consekences. Ez a basis for a settlement, I shell insist on the follerin condishens:

" The Federal debt must be repoodiated, prin- cipal and interest, or ef paid, the Southern war debt must be paid likewise — ez a peece offerin. The doctrine uv State Rites must be made the soopreme law uv the land, that the South may withdraw whenever they feel theirselves dissatisfied with Mas- sachusetts. Uv coarse this is a olive branch.

"Jefferson Davis must be to-wunst set at liberty and Sumner hung, ez proof that the North is really consilliatory.   On this pint I am inflexible, and on the others immovable."

An old man who hed bin listnin to our talk, murmured that there wuz a parallel to this last proposishen.

"Where?" demanded the Genral.

"The Jews, I remember," replied he, "demanded that Barrabas be released unto them, who wuz a thief, I believe, and the Savior be crucified, but I forgit jist how it wuz."

The Genral withered him with a litenin glance, and resoomed:

"I shel, uv course, offer the North suthin in the way uv compensation, for the troo theory uv a Republikin Government is compermise.   On our part we pledge ourselves to kum back, and give the North the benefit uv our kumin back, so long ez Massachusetts condux herself akkordin to our ijees uv what is rite.   But ef this ekitable adjustment is rejected, all I hev to say then is, I shell resign, and the Government may sink without wun effort from me to save it."

I wuz about to give in my experience, when the old man, who wuz sittin near us, broke in agin:

"My name," sed he, "is Maginnis, and I live in

Alabama. I want to say a word to the gentleman from Karliny, and to the wun from Noo Gersey."

" How," retorted I, " do yoo know I'm from Noo Gersey, not hevin spoken a word in yoor hearin?"

" By a instink I hev. Whenever I see a Sutherner layin it down heavy to a indivijouel whose phisynogamy is uv sich a cast that upon beholdin it yoo instinktively feel to see that yoor pocket-handkercher is safe, a face that wood be dangerous if it had courage into it, I alluz know the latter to be a Northern copperhead. The Noo Gersey part I guessed at, becoz, my friend, that State furnished the lowest order uv copperheads of any uv em. Pardon me ef I flatter yoo. But what I wanted to say wuz, that I spose suthen hez happened doorin the past 4 years. I was a original secessionist. Sum years ago I hed a hundred niggers, and wuz doin well with em. But, unforchunitly, my brother died, and left me ez much more land, but no niggers. I wanted niggers enuff to work that land, and spozed ef cut off from the North, and the slave-trade wuz reopened, I cood git em cheaper. Hentz I seceshed. Sich men ez Genral McStinger told me the North woodent fight or I woodent hev secesht, but I did it. I went out for wool and cum back shorn. I seceshed with 100 niggers to git 200, and alas! I find myself back into the old government, with nary a nigger.

"But all this is no excoose for talkin bald non-cents. Yoo old ass," sed he, addressin Genral Mc-Stinger, "yoo talk uv wat yoo will do, and what yoo wont. Hevent you diskivered that yoo are whipped? Hevent you found out that yoo are sub-joogated? Are yoo back into the Yoonyun uv your own free will and akkord? Hevent yoo got a pardon in yoor pockit, which dockyment is all that saves yoor neck from stretchin hemp? Why do yoo talk uv wat South karliny will and wont do? Good Lord! I recollect about a year since South karliny would *never* permit her soil 2 be pollutid by Yankee hirelins, yit Sherman marched all over it with a few uv em, and skarcly a gun was fired at em. So too I recollect that that sed State, wich wuz agoin to whip the entire North, and wich wood, ef over-powered, submit gracefully and with dignity to annihilation, and sich, wuz the first to git down on her marrow bones, and beg for peace like a dorg. Ef yoo intend this talk for the purpose uv skarin the North, beleeve me when I say that the North aint so easy skared ez it wuz. Ef its intendid for home consumption, consider me the people. Ive heard it before, and I'll take no more uv it until my stumick settles. It makes me puke. The fact is we are whipped, and hev got to do the best we kin. We are a goin to pay the Federal debt, and aint goin to pay the confederet debt. Davis will be hung, and serve him rite. States rites is dead, and slavery is abolished, and with it shivelry; and its my opinion the South is a d—d sight better off without either of em. I kin sware, now, after livin outside uv the shadder uv the flag 4 yeres, that I love it! You bet I do. I carry a small one in my coat pocket. I hev a middlin sized one waved by my youngest boy over the family when at prayers, and a whalin big one wavin over my house all the time. I hev diskivered that its a good thing to live under, and when sich cusses as yoo talk uv what yoo will and wont do under it, I bile. Go home, yoo cusses, go home! Yoo, South, and pullin orf your coat, go to work, thankin God that Johnson's merciful enuff to let yoo go home at all, insted uv hangin yoo up like a dorg, for tryin to bust a Guverment too good for yoo. Yoo, North, thankful that the men uv sense uv the North hed the manhood to prevent us from rooinin ourselves by makin sich ez yoo our niggers. Avaunt!"

And the excited Mr. Maginnis, who is evidently subjoogated, strode out uv our presence. His intemperit talk cast a chill over our confidencis, and we dident resoom with the ease and freedom we commenced with, and in a few minutes we parted. I didn't like him.

PETROLEUM V. NASBY,
Lait Paster uv the Church of the New Dispensashun.

III.

A Remarkable Dream. — A Country settled exclusively by Democrats.

Washington, December 1, 1865.

LAST nite I was the victim uv another dream. Ef I don't quit this explorin the realms of the fucher in my sleep, I shall become a second Saint John. Ef so, I maik no doubt my revelations will be uv a remarkably startlin character.

Methawt the Ablishnists had asserted the power we diskivered they possest, after the late elecshuns, and had gone the whole figger. They had forced the South into the humiliashen uv allowin niggers to testify, and in the Northern states had given em the elective franchise. Uv course the edecated and refined democrasy wood never consent to be carried up to the polls alongside uv a nigger — uv course no Democratic offis-seeker wood hoomiliate himself to treatin a nigger afore a election, it bein a article uv faith with us never to drink with a nigger, onless he pays for it.

Therefore, bein helpless, and resolvin never to submit, the heft uv the Democrasy determined to emigrate in a body to some land where the Anglo-Sackson cood rool, — where there was no mixter of the disgustin African. Mexico wuz the country chosen, and methawt the entire party, in one solid column, marched there. Our departure was a ovation. The peeple on our route wuz all dressed in white, ez a token uv joy, and from every house hung banners, with inscriptions onto em, sich ez, —

"Now is our hen-roosts safe!"

"Canada on its way to Mexico!"

"Poor Mexico — we bewail thy fate!"

Our march resembled very much that uv the childern uv Isrel. Our noses wuz the pillers uv fire by nite, and our breath the piller uv smoke by day.

On our arrival to Mexico, the natives of that country, struck probably with awe at the majestic and flamin expression uv our countenances, hastily gathered up their linen, and silver spoons, and hosses, and sich, and retreated to the mountains. It wuz a kompliment to us that them ez hadn't ennything remained.

Finally we reached a plain, where we, the modern childern uv Isrel, decided to remane, and, uv course, the fust thing to do wuz to form a guvernment.

Methawt Fernandy Wood, uv New York, wuz chosen viva voce, ez President, and he stept forerd to hev the oath administered to him, wich wuz 2 be dun by the oldest Justis uv the Peece uv the late stait uv Noo Gersey, wich hez committed sooicide. Here a new trouble ensood — there wuzn't a bible to be found in the whole encampment. The difficulty wuz got over by a New York Alderman yellin out, "Never mind the oath. What's the yoose uv any oath *he* takes?" So he wuz declared President.

Prest. Wood then proceeded to organize. He requested sich ez hed held commissions in the army uv the Yoonited States to step forerd three paces. Gens. Micklelan, Buel, Fitsjohn Porter, & Slocum stept forerd, and with em some 4,000, a part uv whom hed held quartermasters' commissions, and whose accounts,

"Jest afore the battle, mother,"

didn't balance, but wich alluz did jist after, and others who hed bin dismist for bein in the rear, when their sooperiors desired to see em in the front, and who consekently considered it a d—d Ablishun war, wich they didn't approve uv no how.

Then hevin ascertained the material for officerin his army, he axed all them who hed bin in the service as privates to step forerd. 20,000 obeyed, and the President asked the fust one where he enlisted, who ansered ez follows : —

" At Noo York, April 12, 1864, bounty $1,000 ; and at Philadelphia, April 14, 1864, bounty $700 ; and at Pittsburgh, April 16, 1864, bounty $800 ; and at Cincernati, April 19, 1864, bounty $400 ; and at — "

" Enough," said Fernandy, and glancin down the line, and seein all the faces were uv the same style and expression, he asked no more uv em any questions.

Remarkin that it wuz well enough to establish a church, he desired all who were ministers uv the Gospel to step forerd. 21 stept out and desired to explain. They cood not say that they were just now in full connexion with any church. They hed bin, but their unconstooshnel Ablishin Synods and conferences hed accoosed em uv irregularities in hoss tradin, and various other irregularities, and suspended em, and silenced em and sich, becoz they were Democrats, but —

The President shrugged his sholders, and asked all who cood read to step out. About one-half answered, and then he requestid sich uv this number ez cood be prevaled upon to accept a small

office, and who bleeved theirselves fit, to step out
agin, and to my unutterable horror and consterna-
tion, every one but five stepped out ez brisk ez so
many bees. Immejitly there wuz an uproar. Them
ez coodent read swore vociferously that there wuz
nothin fair about *that* arrangement. They never
knowd that a man wuz obliged to be able to read to
hold office in the Democratic party, and they'd never
stand that, and they all stepped out.

Finally it wuz decided that a election should be
held at some fucher time.

The next step wuz to divide em up into employments. The President requested them ez preferred
to foller mekanikle employments to step out: Sum
thirty advanced. Them ez preferred farmin: About
fifty stept out. Them ez expected to run small groceries:

There wuz a sound like the rush uv many waters.
Ninety-eight per cent. uv all — ceptin the officers
and preachers — sprung to the front, but when they
saw ther strength, their faces turned white. "Good
Lord!" whispered they; "we can't make a livin
out uv the remainin two per cent. and the officers
and preachers!"

The mass then demanded a division uv the property, that all mite start alike, but upon takin a in-

ventory, it wuz found not wuth while to bother
about a division.

Then they commenced murmurin, and sed wun
to another, "Oh for the flesh pots uv the Egypt we
left!" "I cood, at hum, live off my Ablishn na-
bers." "There wuz rich men in our ward, but ez
we hed the majority, *they* paid taxes, which *we*
spent!" "Ablishnists is pizen, but it is well enough
to hev enough uv em to tax!" and ez wun man,
they resolved to return, and the confusion that resulted from the breakin up awoke me.

There is onquestionably a moral in the vision.
Ez often ez I hev syed for perpetual Democratic
majorities, I hev sumtimes, when our party wuz
successful, and bid fair to be so permanently, won-
dered what we would do with the Treasury ef we
didn't lose the offices occasionally, so ez to hev the
other party nurse it into pickin condition for us.

I don't think I shood like to live in a unanimous
Dimocratic community.

PETROLEUM V. NASBY,
Lait Paster uv the Church of the Noo Dispensashun.

IV.

A Change of Base— Kentucky.—A Sermon which was interrupted by a Subjugated and Subdued Confederate.

CONFEDRIT X ROADS
(wich is in the Stait uv Kentucky),
December 9, 1865.

HERE in the grate Stait uv Kentucky, the last hope uv Democrisy, I hev pitched my tent, and here I propose to lay these old bones when Deth, who has a mortgage onto all uv us, shall see fit to 4close. I didn't like to leave Washinton. I luv it for its memories. Here stands the Capitol where the President makes his appintments; there is the Post Offis Department, where all the Post-masters is appinted. Here it was that Jaxon rooled. I hed a respex for Jaxon. I can't say I luved him, for he never yoosed us rite. He hated the Whigs ez bad ez we did, but after we beat em and elevated him to the Presidency, the stealins didn't come in ez fast ez we expected. Never shel I forgit the compliment he paid me. Jest after his election I presented myself afore him with my papers, an appli-

3

cant for a place.   He read em, and scanned me with a critic's eye.

"Can't yoo make yoose uv sich a man ez me?" sez I, inquirinly.

"Certinly," sez he; "I kin and alluz hev.   Its sich ez yoo I use to beet the whigs with, and I am continyooally astonished to see how much work I accomplish with sich dirty tools.   My dear sir," sed he, pintin to the door, "when I realize how many sich cusses ez yoo there is, and how cheap they kin be bought up, I really tremble for the Republic."

I didn't get the office I wantid.

Yet ez much ez I love Washinton, I wuz forced to leave it.   I mite hev stayed there, but the trooth is, the planks uv that city and the pavements are harder, and worse to sleep on, than those uv any other city in the Yoonited Staits.   I hed lived two months by passin myself off ez Dimekratic Congress-men, but that cood only last a short time, there not bein many uv that persuasion here to personate.   I had gone the rounds uv the House ez often ez it wuz safe, and one nite commenced on the Senit. Goin into Willard's, I called for a go uv gin, wich the gentlemanly and urbane bar keeper sot afore me, and I drank.   "Put it down with the rest uv mine," sez I, with a impressive wave uv the hand.

Do you know Charles Sumner? Page 35.

"Yoor name?" sez he.

Assoomin a intellectual look, I retorted, "Do you know Charles Sumner?"

Here I overdid it; here vaultin ambition o'er-leaped herself. Hed I sed "Saulsbury," it mite have ansered, but to give Sumner's name for a drink uv gin wuz a peece uv lunacy for wich I kan't account. I wuz ignominiously kicked into the street. Drinks obtained at the expense uv bein kicked is cheep, but I don't want em on them terms; my pride revolted, and so I emigrated. The gentlemanly and urbane conductors uv the Pennsylvania Central passed me over their road. They did it with the assistance uv two gentlemanly and urbane brakesmen, wich dropped me tenderly across the track, out uv the hind eend uv the last car.

I found here a church buildin, uv wich the congregation had bin mostly killed in bushwhackin expeditions, and announsin myself ez a constooshnel preacher from Noo Gersey, succeeded in drawin together a highly respectable awjience last Sunday.

Takin for a text the passage, "The wagis uv sin is death," I opened out ez follows: —

"Wat is sin? Sin, my beloved hearers, is any deviashen from yer normal condishen. Yoor beloved pastor hez a stumick and a head, wich is in close sympathy with each other, so much so, indeed, that the principal biznis uv the head is to fill the stumick, and mighty close work its been for many years, yoo bet. Let yoor beloved pastor drink, uv a nite, a quart or two more than his yoosual allowance, more than his stumick absolootely demands, and his head swells with indignashen. The excess is sin, and the ache is the penalty.

"The wagis uv sin is death! Punishment and sin is ez unseperable ez the shadder is from the man — one is ez shoor to foller the other ez the assessor is to kum around — ez nite is to foller day. The Dimekratic party, uv wich I am a ornament, hez experienced the trooth uv this text. When Douglas switched off, he sinned, and ez a consekence, Linkin wuz elected, and the Sceptre departed from Israel. When — "

At this pint in the discourse, a old man in the back part uv the house ariz and interrupted me. He sed he hed a word to say on that subjick which must be sed, and ef I interrupted him till he got through he'd punch my hed; whereupon I let him go on.

"Trooly," sez he, "the wages of sin is deth. I I hev alluz bin a Dimecrat. The old Dimocracy hez bin in the service uv sin for thirty years, and

the assortment uv death it hez received for wages is
trooly surprisin.   Never did a party commence better.   Jaxon wus a honist man, who knew that right-
eousnis wuz the nashun's best holt.   But he died,
and a host uv tuppenny politicians, with his great
name for capital, jumped into his old clothes, an
undertook to run the party.   Ef the Dimocracy
coold hev elected a honist man every fourth or fifth
term, they mite hev ground along for a longer
period, but alars! Jaxon wuz the last of that style
we hed, and so many dishonist cusses wuz then in
the Capital that his ghost coodent watch the half uv
them.

"The fust installment uv deth we reseeved wuz
when Harrison beet us.   The old pollytishens in
our party didn't mind it, for, sez they, ' The Treas-
urey woodent hev bin wuth mutch to us ennyhow
after the suckin it has experienced for 12 years; it
needs 4 years uv rest.'   We elected Poke, and here
it wuz that Sin got a complete hold uv us.   Anshent
compacts made with the devil wuz alluz ritten in
blud.   We made a contract with Calhoonism, and
that wuz ritten in blud wich wuz shed in Mexico.
Here we sold ourselves out, boots and britches, to
the cotton Democricy, and don't our history ever
sence prove the trooth uv the text, ' The wages uv

sin is deth?' O, my frends! in wat hevy install-
ments, and how regularly, hez these wages bin
pade us.

" Our men uv character commenst leavin us. Silas
Write kicked out, and wood hev gone over agin us
hed he not fortunately died too soon, and skores uv
uthers followed soot. Things went on until Peerse
wuz elected. The Devil (wich is cotton), whom
we wuz servin, brot Kansas into the ring, and wat a
skatterin ensood.

" Agin, the men uv character got out, and gradu-
ally but shoorly the work uv deth went on. Bookannon wuz elected, but wuz uv no yoose to us.
After Peerse hed run the machine four yeers, wat
wuz there left? Eko ansers. Anuther siftin follered, and the old party wich wunst boasted a Jaxon
hed got down to a Vallandigum. The Devil, to
wich we hed sold ourselves, wood not let us off with
this, however. ' The wages uv sin is deth,' and
we hed not reseeved full pay ez yet. He instigated
South Karliny to rebel; he indoosed the other
Democratic States to foller; he forced the Northern
Democrisy to support em, and so on. That wuz
the final stroke. Dickinson. and Cass, and Dix,
and Todd, and Logan, all left us, and wun by wun
the galaxy uv Northern stars disappeared from the

Democratic firmament, leaving Noo Gersey alone, and last fall, my brethrin, she sot in gloom.

" Oh, how true it is! We served sin faithfully, and where are we? We went to war for slavery, and slavery is dead. We fit for a confederacy, and the confederacy is dead. We fit for States Rites, and States Rites is dead. And Democracy tied herself to all these corpses, and they hev stunk her to death.

" Kentucky went heavy into the sin biznis, and whar is Kentucky? We sent our men to the confedrit army, and none uv em cum back, ceptin the skulkers, who comprised all uv that class wich we wood hev bin glad to hev killed. Linkin wantid to hev us free our niggers, and be compensatid for em. We held on to the sin uv niggers, and now they are taken from us with nary a compensate. In short, whatever uv good the Devil promised us in pollytix hez resulted in evil. My niggers is gone, my plantashen here hez fed alternately both armies, ez they cavorted backerds and forrerds through the Stait, my house and barns wuz burnt, and all I hev to show for my property is Confedrit munny, which is a very dead article uv death. I know not what the venerable old sucker in the pulpit wuz a goin to say, but ef he kin look over this section uv the heritage, and cant preach a elokent sermon on that text, he aint much on the preach.   I'm dun."

Uv coarse, after a ebulition of this kind, I cooldn't go on.   I dismist the awdience with a benedick-shun, hopin to get em together when sich prejudiced men aint present.

PETROLEUM V. NASBY,

Lait Paster uv the Church uv the Noo Dispensashun.

V.

The Effect the Proclamation of Secretary Seward produced in Kentucky.

CONFEDRIT X ROADS
(wich is in the Stait uv Kentucky),
December, 20, 1865.

AT last! The deed is dun! The tiranikle government which hez sway at Washington hez finelly extinguished the last glimerin flicker uv Liberty, by abolishin slavery! The sun didn't go down in gloom that nite — the stars didn't fade in2 a sickly yeller, at wich obstinacy uv nachur I wuz considably astonished.

I got the news at the Post Offis (near wich I am at present stayin, at the house uv a venerable old planter, who accepts my improvin conversation and a occasional promise, wich is cheap, ez equivalent for board). Sadly I wendid my way to his peaceful home, dreadin to fling over that house the pall uv despair. After supper I broke to em ez gently ez I cood the intelligence that three-fourths uv the

States hed ratified the constooshnel amendment —
that Seward had ishood his proclamation, and that
all the Niggers wuz free!

Never did I see sich sorrer depicted on human
countenance — never wuz there despair uv sich depth.
All nite long the bereaved inmates uv that wunst
happy but now distracted home wept and waled in
agony wich wuz perfectly heart rendin.

"Wo is me," sobbed the old man, wringin his
hands.

"John Brown's karkis hangs a danglin in the air,
but his sole is marchin on.

"It took posseshun of Seward, and thro his ugly
mouth it spoke the words 'the nigger is free,' and
there is no more a slave in all the land.

"Wunst I hed a hundred niggers, and the men
were fat and healthy, and the wenches wuz strong,
and sum uv em wuz fair to look upon.

"They worked in my house, and my fields, from
the rising uv the sun to the goin down uv the same.

"Wuz they lazy? I catted them till they wuz
cured thereof; for lo! they wuz ez a child under
my care.

"Did they run away? From Kentucky they run
North, and lo! the Locofoco Marshals caught them
for me, and brought them back, and delivered them

into my hand, without cost, sayin, lo! here is thy
nigger — do with him ez thou wilt (wich I alluz
did), wich is cheeper than keepin dogs, and jest as
good.

"Solomon wuz wise, for he hed uv konkebines a
suffishensy, but we wuz wiser in our day than
him.

"For he hed to feed his children, and it kost him
shekels uv gold and shekels uv silver, and much
corn and oil.

"We hed our konkebines with ez great a muchness ez Solomon, but we sold their children for silver, and gold, and red-dog paper."

And all nite long the bereaved old patriarch, who
hed alluz bin a father to his servants (and a grand-
father to menny uv em) poured out his lamentations.

In the mornin the niggers wuz called up, and ez
they all hed their koats on, and hed bundles, I spect
they must hev heard the news. The old gentleman
explained the situation to em.

"Yoo will," sed he, "stay in yoor happy homes
— you will alluz continue to live here, and work
here, ez yoo hev alluz dun!"

The niggers all in korious, with a remarkable
unanimity, remarkt that ef they hed ever bin introdoost to theirselves, they thought they woodent. In

fact, they hed congregated at that time for the purpose uv startin life on their own hook.

A paroxysm uv pain and anguish shot over the old man's face. Nearest to him stood a octoroon, who, hed she not bin tainted with the accurst blood uv Ham, wood hev bin considered beautiful. Fallin on her neck, the old patriarch, with teers a streamin down his furrowd cheeks, ejackilated, —

"Farewell, Looizer, my daughter, farewell! I loved yoor mother ez never man loved nigger. She wuz the solace uv my leisure hours — the companion uv my yooth. She I sold to pay orf a mortgage on the place — she and yoor older sisters. Farewell! I hed hoped to hev sold yoo this winter (for yoo are still young), and bought out Jinkins; but wo is me! Curses on the tirent who thus severs all the tender ties uv nachur. Oh! it is hard for father to part with child, even when the market's high; but, Oh God! to part thus —— "

And the old gentleman, in a excess uv greef, swoonded away genteely.

His son Tom hed bin caressin her two little children, who wuz a half whiter than she wuz. Unable to restrain hisself, he fell on her neck, and bemoaned his fate with tetchin pathos.

Effect of the Emancipation Proclamation in Kentucky. Page 45.

"Farewell, farewell, mother uv my children! Farewell faro, and hosses, and shampane — a long farewell! Your increase wuz my perquisites, and I sold em to supply my needs. Hed you died, I cood hev bin resigned; for when dead you ain't wuth a copper; but to see yoo torn away livin, & wuth $2,000 in enny market — it's too much, it's too much!"

And he fainted, fallin across the old man.

"Who'll do the work about the house?" shreekt the old lady, faintin and fallin across Tom.

"Who'll dress us, and wash us, and wait on us?" shreekt the three daughters, swoonding away, and fallin across the old woman.

My first impulse wuz to faint away myself, and fall across the three daughters; but I restraned myself, and wuz contented with strikin a attitood and organizin a tablo. Hustlin the niggers away with a burnin cuss for their ingratitood, I spent the balance uv the forenoon in bringin on em too. Wun by wun they became conshus; but they wuz not theirselves. Their minds wuz evidently shattered; they wuz carryin a heavy heart in their buzzums.

Wood, Oh! wood that Seward cood hev seen that groop! Sich misery does Ablishinism bring in its trane — sich horrers follers a departure from Dimi-kratic teechins. When will reason return to the people? Eko answers, When?

PETROLEUM V. NASBY,
Lait Paster uv the Church uv the Noo Dispensashun.

VI.

A Conversation with a Loyal Kentuckian, who had Faith in the final Triumph of Democracy.

Confedrit X Roads
(wich is in the Stait uv Kentucky),
January 6, 1866.

I SEE a lite. Democricy is not that dead karkis its enemies hoped for and its friends feared. My noomerious friends here insisted that ez I wuz growin into the seer and yaller leaf, I shood abandon Dimocrisy, and flote with the current. I cant. Ez troo ez the needle to the pole, so am I to Dimocrisy. Young wimmin flock to marryins, middle-aged ones to bornins, and old ones to buryins, which shows concloosively to the most limited intelleck wat the mind uv each class runs upon. So it is with me. To me Dimocrisy is wife, mother, and child.

I hev diskivered many things sense I hev bin in Kentucky — things wich elevated my deprest heart ez yeast does dough, wich filled my shrunken soul ez wind does a bladder.

The people uv Kentucky wuz all loyal. Doorin the horrible fratrisidle war wich hez rent the proud temple uv liberty into twain, they preserved a strict nootrality. I hed a conversation with wun old patriarch, who asshoored me that he hed never taken sides.

Upon his honor, he asshoored me that, after battles, he rifled the corpses uv both armies, impartially. " Cood any boddy be more nootraller than that?" he asked. " My sons," sed he, " wuz in the confedrit army. This fact wood hev turned the affections uv a week-minded man in that direction ; but when I thot uv the boys, I alluz thot also uv that gellorious star-spangled banner, under wich I hed whipped my niggers and sold their children ; under whose shadder I hed men servants, and made servants, and home-made servants born unto me. That banner hed bin my shield. Ef my niggers run off, who so prompt in their pursoot ez the Democratic marshals, wich alluz returned em to me ef it wuz possible? The instooshun wuz guaranteed to me by solemn compermises, wich we cood hev ez often ez we desired. Compermises wuz our best holt. Whenever we wanted anything, all we hed to do wuz to ask for it. The Ablishinists wood object, the Dimocrisy wood draw up a compermise, wich inklooded, ez a rool, twice or 3 times wat we asked, and pass it to save the Union. Sich a Union wuz worth havin, and I opposed all efforts to dissolute it. Hed the South succeeded, I shood hev gone with em ; for Kentucky alone — the only nigger State in the North — wood hev bin helpless. Scaldin tears hev I shed when contemplatin the horrors uv war ; but I cood do nothin to avert it. Kentucky wuz loyal, but nootral."

I find down here that the loyal citizens uv Kentucky who hev returned from the confedrit service are not at all discouraged ; on the contrary, they are hopeful. Sed one to me (I bleeve he wuz a Kernel under Gen. Forest ; indeed, I think he told me he participated in the glorious victory at Fort Piller), —

"Why art thou cast down? Things is workin eggsackly to our hand."

In a mournful tone, I retorted that I failed to perseeve it.

"I kin," sez he. "Lookye, my venerable friend. Is the Northern Dimocrisy still troo?"

"They is," I replied, "wat few remains. But, alas! war, crool war, hez decimated our ranks five times."

"How so?" sez he. "None uv your kind uv

4

Democrats jined in this unholy croosade, and fell afore our deth-deelin swords — did they?"

"Not any," sez I; "but Kanady and Montana took em afore each draft. That wuz why we wuz so beet at the eleckshuns. For one week-kneed Ablishinist we scared into our ranks, we lost two by emigration; and, unfortunitly, wun half that emigrated starved to deth, and tother half is distribbited in the various States prisons in them lands uv refuge."

"Still," sez he, "it matters not. Yoo hev deestricks yoo kin carry in most uv the States. The Five Points deestrick, in Noo York, is ours. Noo Gersey will go back to her allegiance. The new gold States, where so menny uv our friends fled, will send up Democrats to Congress. Ohio hez 2 devoted to us, Pennsylvany hez several, and the most uv the Northern States will send one or two; and them from the North kin be depended on to go any measure we say. Then" — and he slapped me on the back highlariously — "the niggers is free!"

"Well?" sez I, not seein wat cause for highlarity that wuz.

"Well," sez he, "them niggers is not now OTHER PERSONS! We alluz counted five uv em for three in making up the Congressers we wuz entitled to;

now they count as white men, wich increases our
delegashuns to sich an extent that ef yoo Northern
men do half yoor dooty, we'll hev a majority in Congress.   Then, good Lord! the pleasant crack uv the
whip shel agin be heard on the plains uv the sunny
South.   The niggers wont be re-enslaved; but our
Legislaters will speedily redoose em to their normal
condishun.   We shell observe the Constitushnel
Amendment strickly and in good faith.   The Afrikin shel be free; but the good uv society demands
that he shel be under proper guardianship.   He
wont be allowed to change his location; and the
laws uv the States will define his dooties, and give
us the power uv enforcin em.   He wont be allowed
to hev arms, so he can't resist.   Ez he can't leave a
plantation, he will hev to submit quietly to sich rools
ez the high-minded planter makes for him, or be
shot on the spot, or turned out to die uv starvashun,
akording to circumstances.   Ef the planter is a un-
rejenerated child uv damnashun, he will shoot him;
ef he is a saint, who hez a southern hope uv a blessed immortality beyond the grave, he'll restrane his
anger, and turn him out to die uv hunger, onless he
repents, and comes back humble.   Then, they bein
free and responsible for theirselves, we ain't obleeged
to take care uv the sick, the aged, or the infirm, so

97476

it will be really better than it wuz before. I see a gellorious future afore us. Thro the thick clouds uv gloom the brite sun uv hope cheerinly breaks. Say to the Northern Dimocrisy, be uv good cheer. Agin they shel lick our hands; agin they shel eat the crumbs that fall from the National table.

"Thank God for the Northern Dimocrisy, with the other blessins He has given the South. With niggers to do our manual labor for nothing, with Northern Democrats to do our votin at almost the same price, we are trooly a favored people. Bless the Lord for the nigger and the Democrat, wich is both useful to us, each in his speer!"

I drew encouragement from his remarks. The deep vane uv pious thankfulness wich run through his discourse was nateral to him. He is a trooly pious man, and wuz just back frum the meetin uv the Synod uv one uv the Southern churches, wich still persists in quotin Onesimus and Hayger. I feel encouraged. O, Dimmycrats uv the North, let us

"Our vigger renoo,
And our journey pursoo,"

and I feel shoor that success will at last crown our efforts.

PETROLEUM V. NASBY,
Lait Paster uv the Church uv the Noo Dispensashun.

VII.

A Vision. — Celebration of the Anniversary of the Taking of New Orleans. — In the Vision the Spirit of Andrew Jackson appears, and discourses of Various Things.

CONFEDRIT × ROADS
(wich is in the Stait uv Kentucky),
January 12, 1866.

WE had sort uv a celebrashun uv the 8th day uv Janooary at the Corners last nite. My meetin house wuz gorgeously decorated for the occashun; the walls bein hung with confedrit battle flags, and on the corners of the pulpit wuz placed two skulls uv Yankees, picked up at Andersonville by one of the guards, who is now a loyal citizen uv this State, residin at this pint. These skulls wuz illuminated by placin a taller candle inside uv each uv em. The effect wuz inspirin. The guard who contributed em, is, I need not say, a conservative Democrat, and in the matter uv swearing at Ablishnists he displays more talent, and hez a more comprehensive range uv oaths, than any man I ever

NAZARETH COLLEGE LIBRARY

knowed. The church wuz also decorated with
mottoes, furnished by myself and others, uv wich
the followin is some uv em : —

"The Yoonyun ez it wuz — under Bookanan."

"The noble dead uv Kentucky — them ez fell
pintin their guns north we'll alluz remember."

"Our returned soljers — beaten, but not conkered."

"Niggers and northern Dimocrisey — we've lost
the first ; thank God, the latter is ours forever."

I hevn't time nor space to give, in full, the perceedins uv the evenin. Suffice it to say, at 12, precisely, the company broke up, and sich uv em ez
were able, departed. I remained. There wuz suthin
in the refreshments wich indoost me to stay ; in fact,
I coodn't conveniently get out from under the table,
where I hed fallen.

While peacefully sleepin the sleep uv innosence,
my unfettered sole went orf on a explorin expedishen
into the land uv dreams, and I dreamed.

Methawt that we wuz celebratin the anniversary
uv the battle uv Noo Orleans, on a heavier skale
than the wun just closed. We hed, at our festive
board, all the grate lites uv Dimocrisy. There wuz
Fernandy Wood and his brother Ben, and Dan
Voorhes. and the grate Valandigum and Frank

Peerce, and Bookanon hed consented to emerge from his saint-like retirement, and meet with us. The South wuz represented by sich noble Dimocrats ez Yancy, and Toombs, and Wigfall; in short, it wuz a reyoonyun uv old-time Dimocrats, met not only to honor the memry uv Jackson, but to consult ez to the best method uv savin the yoonyun from the rox uv Abolishun onto wich it seems now to be driftin.

The gileless Bookanon wuz President uv the evenin, and Breckinridge Vice President, and toasts wuz drank ez follows: —

" The ancient Dimocrisy — troo to the country, ez long ez there is an office to be filled."

Response by Fernandy Wood.

" The President uv the evenin — the last Dimocratic President uv the Yoonited States."

Mr Bookanan rose to respond, but he wuz overkum, and sank back, his eyes suffoozed with tears. In a voice broken with emoshun, he intimated that he wuz in daily expectation uv bein translated, ez Elijer wuz, in a barouche with two white hosses. " White," he repeated; " for ef the team is black, I won't go; I'll die the nateral way fust." " My frends," sed he, " keep my mantle out uv the hands uv the Jews. Wher is the Elisha who'll wear it?"

" The yoonun ez it wuz, the constooshun ez it is, and the nigger where he ought to be."

Response by Breckinridge, who sed he hed bin four years fightin the battles uv the Dimocrisy, whose prinsiples wuz happily set forth in the senti-ment. Beeten in the field, we must fight it out at the ballot-box. *Nil despritrando* must be the mot-to uv the Dimocrisy.

" Androo Jaxon, the — "

As thus much uv the toast wuz read, there wuz a clap uv thunder heard, wich shook the buildin, and made not only the windows rattle, but the glasses to dance on the table, and the gost uv Androo Jaxson hisself, in the uniform uv 1812, come down through the ceelin. There wuz a frown on his countenance, terrible to behold. Turnin to the company, he remarked that the gate-keeper uv hell must hev slept at his post, for out uv no other Depository cood there be gathered so many villianous counte-nances. " I perpose," sed he, " to respond to this sentiment myself." The Woods slid out uv their seets, under the table ; Breckinridge sneaked out uv the church ; Vallandigham, with his natural impu-dence, tried to face it out, but one look from Androo J. finished him, and he slid, and Bookannon tried to git out, but Androo caught him by the collar, and held him.

"I hev suthin to say to yoo. The chair yoo wunst disgraced, I okkepied, called to it, ez yoo v. uz, by the voice uv the peeple. I swore to preserve the constitooshen and the yoonyun, and so did yoo. I did it, and yoo didn't. When South Carliny undertook to nullify, I bustid the arrangement, becoz I didn't propose to hev the yoonyun I fought for in two wars go down to death, when a particle uv pluck, put in at the right time, cood save it. Yoo mite hev dun the same, but yoo woodent. Yoo took the seat for the purpose of bustin it; for one term of the Presidency yoo agreed to destroy the Government.

"What are yoo here for?" shouted the gost in a terribly sepulkral tone, and a stampin his feet and grittin his teeth. "To celebrate the battle uv Noo Orleans? Yoo stole the livery uv Jaxon to serve Calhoon in. Under the shadder uv my name, yoor dooing deeds wich, ef I wuz in the flesh, I'd hang yoo for. How I wished, in '60 and '61, I cood revisit the earth. I'd hev histed yoo out uv the seat yoo disgraced, and never hev let Linkin hed the credit uv puttin down a rebellion. It wood hev bin lively for some uv yoo. I'd hev ornamented the trees with your karkises; the Southern buzzards wood hev grown fat on secesh korpses.

"Go back, yoo idiots — go back to your first love. Get the wool out uv your teeth, and try to think more uv your country than yoo do uv a yaller girl. Yoo kin yit repent. A. Johnson, whose initials is the same ez mine, runs over with mercy, or he wood hev hung the half uv yoo. Repent and be saved. There is a slite chance for yoo yit. The dyin theef wuz pardoned on the cross, wich ought to be encouragin to yoo, for yoo hev longer time left in wich to repent, and the Lord knows yoo need it. But ef yoo will go on in yer iniquity, do it on yoor own hook. Don't take my name in vain no more. I hevn't nothin in common with yoo, nor never had. Yoo yoosed to follow me, the same ez a drove uv jackals alluz follers a lion, to devour the hides, and bones, and offal that he despises. The lion hez gone hentz, and yoor takin his skin, and are trying to imitate his roar. The skin hangs loose upon yoo, and the roar is a miserable squeak. Never let me hear of yoor celebratin any more uv my doins. I go."

And in another clap of thunder, the gost ascendid through the roof agin.

I awoke. A cold sweat wuz a standin on my intellectooal brow, and a mortal shiverin shook me.

I wuz alone in the church, under the table where I originally fell, and around me wuz skattered, in confusion, the remnant uv the feast. I thot to myself, ef sich wuz the effect uv a dream uv the gost Jaxon, wat wood ensoo ef he shood be raised from the dead, and visit the Dimocrisy in the flesh. Then wood my prayer be continooally, " Good Lord, deliver us."

PETROLEUM V. NASBY,

Lait Paster uv the Church uv the Noo Dispensashun.

VIII.

A Plan suggested for the Up-building of the Democracy.—The Idea not New, but one which the Leaders of the Fierce Democracy have acted upon from the Beginning.

CONFEDRIT X ROADS
(wich is in the Stait uv Kentucky),
January 27, 1866.

HALLELOOGY! halleloogy! halleloogy! I see a lite! It beams onto me! It penetrates me! It fills me! Goy to the world!

I hev diskivered the cause uv the decline uv the Dimocrisy. I seed it yisterday. I wuz a wanderin on the neighborin hills, a musin onto the cussednis uv humanity ez exemplified in the person uv the grocery keeper at the Corners, who unanimusly refoozed to give me further credit for corn whisky, wich is the article they yoose in this country to pizen theirselves with. He asshoored me that he hed the utmost regard for my many virtues; but he diskivered that the one he prized the most I hedn't so many uv, to wit, that uv payin for my likker.

Therefore the account mite be considered closed. Then, for the fust time in my life, I bleeved in total depravity.

While musin, in a melonkoly mood, on this dark cloud wich fell across my pathway, and the fall uv the Dimocratic party, I came onto a party of men borin for ile. Then the trooth flashed over me. Their operations showed me the way to success — the shoor path to triumph.

" When," said I to myself, " when men seek gain they bore for it. They go down — never up. Even so with the Dimocrisy. We dug downward, downward, downward, through all the strata uv society. We went through the groceries; the next stratum was the most ignorant uv the furiners; then we struck the poor whites uv the South; then, below them, the heft uv the people uv Noo Gersy; then Southern Illinoy and Indiana; then Pike county, Missouri; and so on. We never went upward for converts, cause 'twant no use. When a man wanted to jine us he alluz hed to come down. We got lots of converts.

There was a regular slidin scale, which the heft uv Democrats who wuznt born in the party hev slid down; to wit: —

Quarter dollar smiles.

15 cent nips.

10 cent drinks.

5 cent sucks.

A flat flask conceeled.

A bottle openly.

Dimocrisy.

We lost our hold for two reasons. First, the poor likker we hev now kills off our voters too fast; and the tax on whiskey forced two thirds uv our people to quit suckin, and ez soon ez they begun to git on their feet they jined the Ablishnists. Secondly, our leaders spozed there wuz no lower stratum to dig into, and give up in disgust.

But I hev deskivered that lower stratum — I hev found it; and when the idea flashed over my Websterian intelleck, I shouted Halleloogy! The nigger is the lower stratum; and ef we bore down to it, and work it thoroughly, we hev, at least, a twenty years' lease uv power.

We must cultivate the nigger. HE MUST HEV THE SUFFRAGE! It is a burnin shame, that, in this Nineteenth Sentry, in the full blaze uv intelligence, livin under a Deklarashun which declares all men "free and ekal," that a large body uv men shood be denied the glorius privilege uv bein taken up to the poles and voted. Is not the Afrikin a man? Is he

not taxed ez we are, and more than most uv the Democrisy, for many uv em own property? Is he
not amenable to all the laws, even ez we is? Then
why, I triumphantly ask, is he not entitled to a vote?
Ah! why, indeed?

" But this is Ablishnism !" methinks I hear a obtoose Dimocrisy observe in horrer. " And why give
them votes who will use em agin us?"

My gentle friend, *will* they use their ballot agin
us? Ef I know myself, I think not. Kin they read?
Kin they write? Aint the bulk uv em rather degraded and low than otherwise? Methinks. Aint
that the kind uv stock we want, and the kind wich
hez alluz set us up? Readin hez alluz bin agin us.
Every skool master is a engine uv Ablishnism ;
every noosepaper is a cuss. General Wise, uv Vir-
ginia, when he thanked God there wuzn't a noosepaper in his deestrick, hed reason to ; for do yoo
spoze a readin constitooency wood hev ever kept
sich a blatherskite ez him in Congress year after
year?

Then, agin, the Constooshnal Amendment will
pass, givin representashen to voters alone. The
Democratic States will hev more members uv Congress and more electoral votes than afore the war ;
and them States we kin depend on.

But my skeem is still more comprehensive. Them niggers ain't needed in the South. We'll send em North. A few thousand will overbalance the Ablishun majority in Noo Gersey; fifty thousand will bring Ohio back to the fold; the same number will do for New York and Pennsylvany, and the country is saved — we will be able to elect the President. Thus the pit the Ablishnist dug for us he'll fall into hisself; the club he cut for us will break his own head.

Honey hez kum out uv the carcass; good hez perceded from Nazareth. The nigger smells sweeter to me now than Nite bloomin Serious; he is more precious to me than gold, or silver, or preshus stones. He is the way, and I shel walk in it. He shel lift me into a Post orifis. We must give our Afrikin brother, — for is he not a man and a brother? — not only the suffrage, but he must hev land, and the Democracy must give it to him. I want Garrit Davis to instantly interdoose a bill into the Senit givin each family a quarter section uv land, a pair uv mules, and a cook stove; and each female Afrikin brother two flarin calico dresses and a red bonnet. I want him to advocate the bill in a speech uv not more than two hours, so that it will stand some chance uv passin. On second thought, I guess some other man hed better interdoose the bill, as the Sennit hez got into sich a habit uv votin down everything he proposes, that they'd slather this without considerin it, on jineral principles.

Then we've got em. Work ez hard ez they may at it, it'll take twenty years afore the Ablishinists kin edjukate em up to the standard uv votin their tikkit; and even that time won't do it if we kin git the tax taken off uv whiskey, so that we kin afford to use it ez in the happy days uv yore.

Goyusly I went home to lay the foundashun uv the new temple uv Dimocrisy. I slept that nite atween two niggers, and hev bin shakin hands and enquirin after the health uv the families uv all I hev met. Its rather hard for an orthodox Democrat. Sich sudden shifts is rather wrenchin on the conshence. But what uv that? The Dimocrat who hez follered the party closely for thirty years ought not to balk at sich a triflin change ez this, pertiklerly when it promises sich glorious results.

> "There's a lite about to gleem,
>   There's a fount about to streem,
>   Wait a little longer!"

PETROLEUM V. NASBY,
Lait Paster uv the Church uv the Noo Dispensashun.

5

IX.

Enjoys a Vision of the Next World, seeing therein many Curious Things, which are published as a Warning to Politicians.

CONFEDRIT × ROADS
(wich is in the Stait uv Kentucky),
February 5, 1866.

LAST nite I retired to my virtoous couch, at precisely half past eleven, after eatin a rather light supper for that time uv night.   I alluz make it a pint to eat light in the evenin, for I'm gittin old, and my digestive faculties ain't what they was when I wuz young.   Alas! we who hev lived out the best part uv our days, wat wood we give to be set back to the time when, with our faculties unimpaired, we cood consoom a good square meal without fear uv consekenses!   But

"Them happy days is fled,
And never will return."

I paid my respecks to 2 mince pies, a pair uv pig's feet, some cold tongue, and a plate uv tripe,

Nasby's Dream of the Future of Democracy. Page 67.

follered by a half dozen dough nuts and a couple or more uv glasses uv hot whisky punch; and singler ez it may seem, it didn't set well. I dreamed all night, and my dreams wuznt at all pleasant. Methawt I hed deceest, and wuz in the next world. It was a singler site that met my vision. The dividin line atween this world and the next wuz a swift stream uv water, and every deceest spirit hed to cross it. The water wuz suthin like that uv the Dead Sea. A man, unencumbered with anything, cood walk on it, but they sunk down in it if they wuz loaded, accordin to what they hed to carry. On the tother side uv this Jordan wuz heaven; the dominions uv his majesty Satan the 1st wuz below, and to it a strong under current flowed, which took all them ez wuz too heavy loaded to keep their chins above water.

On the bank stood more than two millions uv little devils, who flung onto the shoulders uv them tryin to cross their failins, and weaknesses, and iniquities.

General Breckinridge wuz the first that I saw enter the flood. He hed on a life preserver, labelled " States Rights," but a peert little devil stuck a pin into it, and it collapsed, the gas with wich it wuz filled smellin horribly. Down he went, and ez he sunk, they commenced peltin him with packages labelled " Treason," " Perjury," and " Murder," and John C. went under.

Old James Buckanon went next. The old gentleman didn't keep above water as long ez a able bodied man could hold a bar uv red hot iron in his hand. He made one splash, when a weight labelled " Treason " struck him, and down he went. The gentlemanly and urbane devil who had him in charge had a big pile more uv ammunition to discharge at him, but that one wuz sufficient.

Vallandigham come next. I wuz surprised to see no one make a motion at him, but he sunk all the same. " We never waste effort," sed Satan to me ; " he carries enough natural cussedness about him, all the time, to sink him, without pilin any devilment on his shoulders wich is ten days old."

Frank Peerce made his appearance, but declined to enter. He wuz immediately seezed, and on each leg wuz tied a weight labelled " Kansas," and they flung him in. He went down like a shot, and that's the last I seed uv him.

Garret Davis went in, and to my surprise, passed over safely. Nothin wuz flung at him, for wich I asked the reason.

" Why," sed Satan, " the poor old man isn't accountable. He commenced to talk many years ago, and keeps on talkin because he really don't know when to stop. I could hev sunk him, but the fact is, I woodent endoor what the Senit uv the Yoonited States hez hed to, for the past few years, for a dozen uv Tombs lawyers. Besides this, I'm gettin more from Kentucky now than I am really entitled to. I've a mortgage on two-thirds uv that State."

Fernandy and Ben Wood come up rather bold, and entered the flood ez though they were sure uv goin through all right. With a inimitable chuckle, Satan motioned away the inexperienced devils, and sed, " Leave em to me," and at Ben he hurled a package uv the New York News, wich swashed him down instanter. Jest ez Fernandy wuz beginnin to reach the other shore, he flung onto him an assortment uv weights, labelled " Lotteries " and " Riots," which took him down to the arm pits, and finished by tumblin onto him a mass, onto wich wuz written " Mayoralty," and down he went; at wich His Majesty drew a sigh uv relief.

Seein the style uv the men who sunk, I remarked unto him, —

" This war hez bin a rather profitable thing for you."

" Nothin to speek uv," sed he. " The leaders uv

the Southerners were, sum uv em, honest, and got
through on that account, and the rank and file were
ignorant wretches, who ain't accountable, no how.
The leading copperheads uv the North were mine,
anyhow, from the beginnin. Any man who cood
sympathize with the rebels in sich a struggle, must,
yoo will acknowledge, hev hed a long career uv iniquity to fit em for sich a sin. Why," sed he, " do
yoo think I use all the shot I hev? Not any. Them
yoove seen piled on were used because, bein the
last, they were on the top uv the pile.

"Any quantity uv yoor party escaped me. Them
fellows who are yet votin for Jackson I'll never git,
and the most uv them ez alluz votes unscratched
tickets will dodge me. Their innocence protects
em. It takes a modritly smart man to be vishus
enuff to come to me ; he hez to hev sense enuff to
distinguish between good and evil, cussednis enuff
to deliberately choose the latter, and brains enuff to
do suthin startlin in that line. Dan Voorhees, uv
Injeany, hez all these qualities developed to a degree
wich excites my profound respect. Between him
and Fernandy Wood its nip and tuck. Fernandy
did wicked things with more neatnis than Voohees,
but for a actual love uv doin em Voohees beets the
world. I sed," continued he, " that the war wuzn't

uv much yoose to me. I repeat it; it wuz a damage. Afore the war, I hed my own way, pretty much, in the Southern States. For every octoroon, I cood count on at least two planters, and under the patriarkle system uv Afrikin slavery (wich, by the way, wuz one uv my most brilliant consepshuns), octooroons multiplied with a rapidity pleasin to behold. But now, alas! the octooroon bizness is done, and my best holt is gone. I hev some little hope, however. The Dimocrisy are displayin a vigger I didn't think they possest. Ef they kin only git strength enuff to elect the next President and re-establish slavery! The thought fills me with unutterable joy. The redoosin of the nigger to bondage agin wood give me a clean title to evry last one who helped to do it, and in gittin em back into their normal condishun (by the way, that's another phrase uv mine), ther'd be enuff slaughterin and murders to satisfy several sich Satans ez I am. I'd help em ef I knowd how, but I can't improve on either their speekers or writers, and ez long ez men will do my work gratis, I don't see the yoose uv interferin."

At this pint a couple uv small imps undertook to push me into the stream, and in the struggle, I awoke. My dreem wuz o'er, but the impreshun remained. " Kin it be," mused I, pensively, " that

we are doin the devil's work, and are we to be
finally rewarded in the manner I saw in my vision?
Ef so, hedn't I better quit and repent?"

But I thought agin, that however it mite be for
younger men, it wood be uv no yoose for me. I
hed voted the strait ticket for thirty years, and the
ten or twelve years I hed to live wuz too short a
time in which to repent successfully uv sich iniquity.
So I sank into sleep agin, this time dreemin that I
had turned Fenian — hed elected myself Hed Cen-
ter for the Stait uv Kentucky, and wuz just investin
$75,000 in a magnificent plantashun.

PETROLEUM V. NASBY,
Lait Paster uv the Church uv the Noo Dispensashun.

x.

SONNIT

Onto a Soldier, wich wuz wunst a Dimekrat, but is now a howlin Ablishnist, wich I saw a limpin about on one Leg, hevin left the other at Antee-tam.

BLOO–KOTED monster! thou wentest forth
  Armed with thy rifle and sharp-pinted bayonet,
    Whose peeked eend with Southern blood is wet:
I hate thee, tool and minyun uv the North!
Thou wast a Dimekrat: them kote and pants,
    The wavin flag, the gun with peeked eend,
    Turned yoo into a Abolishn feend,
Who sucked the blood uv Dimekratic saints.
  Monster unnachral! by niggerism hatched,
    Thousands and more uv Dimokrats yoo've slain,
    Who'll never rally to the poles again
To vote, ez wunst they did, a tikkit all unskratched.
    Avant! the work yoo did our party is undoin:
    To us yoor kote uv bloo is jest bloo rooin!

XI.

The Situation.—The Attempt of the President to wheedle Democrats into Supporting his Policy without giving them the Offices commented upon.—The Democracy warned.

CONFEDRIT X ROADS
(wich is in the Stait uv Kentucky),
February 15, 1866.

I HEV had hopes uv Androo Johnson. My waitin sole hez bin centred onto him for a year back. He wuz the Moses wich I spected wood lead the Democrisy out uv the desolate Egypt into which we hev bin making bricks without straw for five long weary and dreary years. O, how I hev yearned for Johnson! O, how I hev waited, day after day, and week after week, and month after month, for some manifestation uv Dimocrisy wich is satisfactory — suthin tangible — suthin that I cood take hold on.

Faith is the substance uv things hoped for, and the evidence of things not seen ; wich is all right so fur

ez religion ez concerned, but uv no account in poli-
tix. A friend uv mine, who wuz a monomaniack
on the subjick uv faith, undertook to live on it, under the insane belief that ef a man had faith pork
wuz unnecessary. Wuz the experiment a success?
Not any. When he commenst the trial he weighed
200; in a week he wuz down to 125; and in four-
teen days he slep in the valley!

I hev bin livin on faith for a year or more, and I
too am thin. My bones show; light shines through
me; I am faint and sick. Oh, for suthin that I can
see and feel — suthin solid!

Our Dimocratic noosepapers are supportin Androo Johnson. They claim that his polisy is our
polisy; that he is ourn, and we are hizn. They are
singin hosanners to him. At his every act they exclaim Halleloogy! in chorus. What is it all about?
In what partikeler hez Androo Johnson showed hisself to be a Dimokrat? In the name uv Dimocrisy
let me ask, "WHERE IS THE OFFICES?" Who's
got em? What is the politikle convickshuns uv the
wretch who is post master at the Corners, and who
only last nite refused, in the most heartless manner,
to trust me for postage stamps? Who is the Collectors, the Assessors, et settry? Are they constitooshnel Dimokrats? Is Stanton, and Seward, and

Welles histed out uv the cabinet, and Vallandigum, and Brite, and Wood apinted in their places? Not onct. Every post master, every collector, every assessor, every officer, is a ablishinist, dyed deeply and in fast colors.

Faith without works is a weak institution; its like a whisky punch with the whisky omitted, wich is a disgustin mixter uv warm water and sugar. What is it to me (who hev bin ready to accept any position uv wich the salary wuz sufficient to maintain a individooal uv simple habits) who is beheaded, so ez I don't get a place? Androo Johnson may cut off offishl heads ez dexterously and proofoosely ez he chooses; but my sole refuses to thrill when I know that Ablishnists, though uv a different stripe, will be apinted. So long ez Dimocrats are kept out, what care I who hez the places? Paul may plant and Apollus water; but uv what account is the plantin and waterin to me ef I don't get the increase? I take no delight in sich spectacles. Ef Androo Johnson proposes to be a Dimockrat, — ef he desires the honest, hearty support of the party, — let him seel his faith with works.

I visited Washington with the express purpose uv seein the second Jackson. I am a frank man, and I laid the matter afore him without hesitation. I told

him that the Postmaster at the Corners wuz opposin
his policy and aboosin him continually; that it wuz
a outrage that men holdin place under the Administration should not sustain the Administration. In
the name uv Right, I demanded a change.

I sposed that to wunst the position would be offered to me; and after protestin a sufficient time
that I did not wish it, and would prefer the apintment of some more worthy man, I should accept it,
and go home provided for three years. Imagine my
deep, my unutterable disgust, when he told me that
he wood investigate the matter, and probably wood
make a change, PROVIDED HE COULD FIND, IN THE
VICINITY, SOME ORIGINAL UNION MAN WHO WOULD
ACCEPT THE PLACE!

Then the iron entered my soul. Then I felt that
in him we had no lot nor part.

Our principles are uv a very comprehensive nature. We are willin to endorse Andro Johnson, or
any other man. We will endorse his theories uv
Reconstruction, or any man's theories. We are
elastic, like Injy rubber. The boy who set a hen on
a hundred eggs acknowledged to his maternal pa-
rent that she could not kiver em; but he remarked
he wanted to see the old thing spred herself. We
have that spreadin capacity. We kin accommodate

the prejudices uv the people uv all the various local-
ities.   In Connecticut we are singin John Brown's
body lies a mouldrin in the grave, in a modritly loud
tone, and supporting a Ablishnist who voted for
doin away with slavery in the District of Columby
and for the Constooshnel Amendment.   In Kentucky we are hangin men uv the John Brown style,
and mobbin all uv the persuasion uv the Connecticut
nominee.   Sich a variety uv principle, — a party uv
sich adaptibility, — kin hev but one great central
idee, on wich there is no diversity uv opinion, and
to which all other ideas is subordinate.   That idea
is POST OFFICE ! and ef Androo Johnson could be
got rite on that question, we'd care not wat else he
required uv us.

We hev our arms around Androo.   We are hug-
gin him to our buzzums ; but he hez left his baggage
to hum.   That baggage is wat we want ; and we
shel fling him off shortly, onless he changes his
policy in this respeck.   He kin hev us on easy
terms ; but he must furnish the ammunishun with
which to fight his battles.   Will he do it ?   That's
the question a hundred thousand hungry soles, who
hanker even ez I do, are daily askin.

PETROLEUM V. NASBY,
Lait Paster uv the Church uv the Noo Dispensashun.

XII.

The President's 22d of February Speech. — The Account thereof of One behind the Scenes. — Hopes and Fears of the Democracy.

WASHINGTON, February 23, 1866.

I DON'T know; but there is a still small voice within me wich whispers, " All is well ! " The delusive phantom, Hope, may be playin false with me. The wish may be paternal parient to the thought, and I may be indulgin in a dream from wich I shel be, to-morrer, roodly awakened; but it's my opinion that the day-star uv glory hez arozen onto the Dimocracy; that our night uv gloom is over; and that, at larst, the Government, or at least the only part we care about, — the offisis, — is ourn. I heerd Androo Johnson speak last nite ! I stood beside him ! I helpt hold him up ! I SMELT HIS BREATH. It's all rite !

I hed hopes when he vetoed that large and varied assortment uv Ablishn abominashens, — the Freed-

men's Burow bill, — notwithstandin there were
pints in his message I coodent sanction. The veto
wuz heavenly, but his reasons were unsound.
When he expressed hisself ez bein determined
upon sekoorin the niggers in their rites, I felt
fearful that there wuz a honist diffrence uv opinion
atween him and Congress wich mite be settled,
and then what wood become uv us? Ef the niggers is to hev rites, in the name uv Heaven, I asked
myself, what difference does it make to us whether
they hev em by Charles Sumner's system (on whose
head rest cusses!), or A. Johnson's? And ez is
customary when men ask theirselves questions, I got
no answer. Men never ask theirselves questions
wich kin be answered.

But last nite my doubts wuz removed. Little
Sam Cox, and Dan Voorhees, and the Woods, and
Tom Florence, and Coyle, and me, hed bin with
Androo all day. The Ablishnists avoided him after
the veto; and knowin he'd done suthin he wuzn't
quite shoor wuz wise, he needed bracin up, and we
wuz ready to brace him. Isn't it singler that men,
when they go to the devil, alluz go in squads? Cox
hed him cornered all day, a readin to him extrax
from Forney's Press, and choice selections from
Sumner's speeches; and Voorhees and the others

wuz a intimatin to him that only in the buzzum uv
the Dimocrisy cood he find that conjeniality uv
sperit so nessary to him; and by the time the ser-
enade wuz ready, he wuz ez full uv venom ez wuz
possible, and his capassity in that line is immense.

The company all went with him onto the stand,
and my eyes saw the first cheerin vision wich they
hev beheld for years. Before us stood ten thousand
or more Dimocrats. There wuz the veteran from
Lee's army in his soot uv gray, which hed, by continyood contact with the pavements uv Washington
— wich, not hevin bin slept on much, sense Bookannon's time, they don't sweep — hed become somewhat uv the color uv the clay. There wuz the offi-
ser who surrendered with Johnston, and them noble
sons uv Baltimore, and Rawly, and Charleston,
who, though they didn't serve their section in the
field, were ardent in their support uv the cause.
There were the old-style Dimocrats uv the North,
whose faith in Johnson's Dimocrisy, based upon the
scene wich took place at the inauguration, wuz
greater than mine, hed come on with their applications for Post Offises, and who jined so heartily in
the cheers wich went up for J. Davis: and there,
addressin this crowd, wuz a President — the man

6

who had the appintin power in his hands — who
cood make and unmake Post Offisis.

It did me good, and yet I doubtid. Wood he go
through with it? Wood he lock horns with Wade
and Sumner, and dare the wrath uv Thad Stevens?
Wood he? He wavered and shrunk back ez he
saw the style uv the awdience before him; for he
hed bin, for four years, accustomed to better dressed
people. But Cox and Florence wuz ekal to the
emergency. Samyooel whispered into his one ear,
" Whitewash !" and Florence into tother, " Charles
the I. !'" and flamin up like a conflagratid oil well,
he waded it. Then I felt that it wuz all right.
Then my soul expanded; and ez he went on, pilin
Billinsgate upon Billinsgate, usin Tennessee stump
slang, improved by a liberal mixter uv the more
desprit variety he hed picked up in Washinton and
Baltimore, I felt that it wuz indeed well with us.
He wuz talkin ez a Dimokrat to Dimokrats; and it
wuz appreciated. Strippin off all uv the disguise
he hed bin a wearin for four years, — washin off, in
rage and whisky, the varnish and putty with wich
he hed shined up his dullness, and filled up the
cracks and cavities wich hed alluz troubled him, —
he stood forth ez we knowd him — Androo Johnson !
How he did froth and foam ! How he did lash his

late associates! and how those Dimokrats who
kum to Washinton with petitions for places in their
pockets did wink at each other, and poke each other
in the ribs, with exultation and jockelarity wich
they cood not conceal! And how the Ablishnists,
wich hung onto the outskirts uv the crowd, in the
hope that he wood declare himself in sich a way
ez to give em some hope, did walk away sorrowfully and sore, ez tho they felt that they hed a new
trouble afore em! And how the soljers uv Lee, and
the quartermasters wich hed made Richmond their
headquarters doorin the war, did cheer and sling
their hats into the air, and in the uncontrollable
enthoosiasm uv the moment invariably snatch better ones from the heads uv the Northern men in the
crowd! It wuz gorgus.

While His Eggslency's course gives me hope, I
don't want it to be understood that I am prepared to
fully and entirely indorse him. I don't go much on
men who do things in a state uv madnis; neither do
I invest heavy in that Dimokrat wich requires an
extra load uv likker to make him act and talk like a
Dimokrat. Androo Johnson was and is a Dimokrat — a ginooine Dimokrat. The accident uv his
learnin to read, in his yooth, gave him a preëmi-
nence over us in Tennessee, and put him through

the various places he hez filled. His affinities wuz
with us; his style wuz our style, and his habits our
habits; and he hed no biznis to ever git out uv the
fold. I cannot forgit that he went back on us at a
critikle time in the histry uv the party. He saw
that the effort the Dimocrisy uv the South wuz
makin to regain their rites wood be a failyoor;
the aristocracy uv the South hed snubbed him, and
refoozed to recognize him; but all this shood not
hev affected him. It's the normal condishn uv the
lower grade uv Dimokrats to be snubbed; and they
hev no rite to inquire whether anything the aristocracy uv the party propose is goin to be a failyoor
or not. It's their dooty to obey orders without ques-
tionin.

Wat spiled Johnson wuz Massachoosits. He pre-
tended to be loyal, and Massachoosits patted him
on the back. They took him into good society.
They let him associate with Sumner and sich, and
the man became infatooated. He got to drinkin high
priced drinks, and wearin clean shirts, and begun to
ape the manners uv those into whose sphere he hed
bin thrown. There wuz these two opposin forces
contendin within him — nateral proclivities and acquired tastes — wich may be represented by whiskey
out uv a jug, and mint jooleps at Willard's. Mas-

sychoosits wuz a pullin him up, and North Carolina wuz equally vigorously pullin him down. He wantid to stay with Massychoosits, but he wuz uncomfortable all the time ; and finally nacher asserted her supremacy, and he broke over, and like the water long confined in a dam, when its bustid its obstructions, and goes, it goes with a loosenis, and tears up, and takes a very large quantity uv dirt and drift wood with it.

Before I tie myself to A. J., I want to know fer certin what he proposes to do. WHO IS TO HEV THE POST OFFISIS? Is Ablishnists to still retain the places uv trust and profit? Does he propose to organize a new party, made up uv sich Republikins ez he can indoose to foller him and the Dimocrisy? Ef so, I ain't in. Decidedly, I ain't in. Emphatically, count me out. For the reason, that he kin git jist enuff Republikins, percisely, and no more, to fill the offisis, and they will be uv sich a character ez will do the Dimokrisy no credit. I won't be tail to no kite. We are willin to play kite ; but tail, never ! Ef we boost Androo Johnson, Androo Johnson must boost us. Does he think we kin carry sich a load ez he is for nothin? Nary. Ef we hev a consoomin desire to git along without offisis, we are doin very well at that now, we

thank you; and we haven't the responsibility uv
the Administration uv a eggstremely shaky man to
carry. Sich loads must be paid for.

But, after all, I hev hopes. He hez cut hisself
loose from Sumner and Stevens; and in less than a
week every Republikin uv modrit sensibilities will
be aboozin uv him to that extent that he won't be
able to git back agin. He's an animal uv the bull
kind; and criticism and opposition is to him the
red flag wich the Spanish matadors, I bleeve they
call em, waves afore the animals they wish to infoo-
riate, and they may drive him into our ranks.

I wait, and watch, and hope. Ef I kin wunst git
a commission, with the broad seel uv the Postmaster
General onto it, confirmin me in the possession uv
the Post orifis at the Corners, I shel bless the day
that Androo Johnson left us, and prokoored his ele-
vation to the Presidency. May the day be hastened!

PETROLEUM V. NASBY,
Lait Paster uv the Church uv the Noo Dispensashun.

XIII.

Another Warning.—Profuse Expenditure of Powder and Torchlight Processions deprecated.— The President implored to show his Hand.

CONFEDRIT X ROADS
(wich is in the Stait of Kentucky),
February 29, 1866.

I NOTICE, all over the North, the Democrisy is a firin guns, and marchin after brass bands, and hirin halls for endorsin Androo Johnson. Ez a sentinel on the watch-tower, I protest!

In the name uv suffrin Kentucky, uv wich State I am a adopted sitizen, I protest!

In the name uv common sense and ordnary politikle sagassity, I protest!

Androo Johnson may possibly be on the high road to Dimocrisy; but, ez yet, what ashoorence hev we? Am I datin my letters from "Post Orifis, Confedrit X Roads?" Hez there bin, as yit, any well authenticated case uv the removal uv a Ablishnist, and the apintment uv a constooshnel Democrat in his stead?

Not that I hev heard of. Per contrary, the Ablishnists — them ez wuz apinted by Linkin — are still
holdin on, ez calm ez a summer mornin, without
any apparent fear uv any change affectin them.

Who pays for the Halls? Who pays the music?
Who pays the Powder? Dimocrats who do these
scent Post Offises in the distance. Are they like the
the war hoss in Job's writins, who smelled the battle afar off, and remarked Ha, Ha! to the trumpets?
Let me enticet sich that they kin make a better in-
vestment uv their means.

The cost uv one meetin, put in korn whisky, wood
not only solace theirselves, but start half a dozen
Ablishnists on the road to Dimocrisy.

Men is deceptive. I hev hopes uv Androo Johnson myself, and principally becoz Vallandigum and
Fernandy Wood hev hopes. Them buzzards kin
smell carrion a long distance, and they are seldom
at fault. In this case, they may be. They base their
hopes on Johnson's speech, at Washington, on the
22d. There may be suthin in it; but ain't it possible
that the stench wich they took for Dimocrisy, and
wich they sposed cum from Johnson, ariz from them
ez surrounded him?

"But," sez a Dimocrat, whose nose, from long
continued lack of supplies, hez softened down from

a generous crimson to a ghastly bloo, and who woodent hev a small Post orifis at no price, ef it wuznt offered him, " look at the class he spoke to."

Wat noncents! Androo wuz mad. There wuz a mass uv bile on hiz politikle stumick wich must be got rid uv. He had sum nasty things to say, and it wuz a part uv the eternal fitness uv things that he shood hev a nasty audience to say em to.

I don't propose to go orf into spasms over the present sitooashun. Johnson proposes to continoo the Freedmens' Buro, and hezn't no noshun of re-peelin the test oath, or uv drawin the military out uv the Dimocratik States. So far as heard from, we uv the South is still in a stait of abject custitood. Our habis corpuses wich Linkin took away from us hevn't bin returned, and we are obleeged to git along ez best we kin without em. I knocked down a small nigger yisterday, for the purpus uv assertin the sooperiority uv the Cauchashun race over the Afrikin, and wuz to wunst hauled up afore a Freed-men's Buro, and fined. Our high-toned and chival-rous members are exclooded from Congris on the frivolus plea that they wuz kernels and briggydeer Ginerals in the Confederit servis ; and all these outragis agin Dimocrisy Androo Johnson, by permittin, absolootly approves.

I could probably swaller all these things. I am a Dimokrat uv thirty years standin, and, uv course, hev bin on both sides uv every politikle fence. The seats of my politikle pants is full of slivers. But, before I take down these things, I WANT TO KNOW WHAT I AM GOIN TO GIT FOR IT. Ef Androo Johnson goes back on his party and his pledges, he, uv course, asks us to go back on ourn. In sich transactions, where both parties, by bein engaged in it at all, confess themselves ruther a low grade of skoundrels, I think it well enuff to hev the consideration paid down.

Ef Androo Johnson wants me, he knows the terms. I am his to command, for a consideration; ez much so ez is the thousands uv Demokrats who hev bin, for the past week, gittin up Demonstrations. But I want suthin to go on. When I hev his permisson, under the broad seel uv the Post Orfis Department, to write "P. M." after my illustrious name, I shell be prepared to wade in. I hev bin huntin up several reasons for supportin him. I hev em all ready. I only want this additional one, and then I fling my banner to the breeze. Faith is sed to be the sun of all religious systems. POST OFFIS is the central figger in all Democratic creeds — the theme uv conversation by day, and the staple uv dreems by night. How long! oh, how long!

PETROLEUM V. NASBY,
Lait Paster uv the Church uv the Noo Dispensashun.

XIV.

Refuses to Support the President, having no Confidence in Him. — Again warns the Democracy.

CONFEDRIT X ROADS
(wich is in the Stait uv Kentucky),
March 12, 1866.

THE politikle sky is orecast with friteful clouds. Darkness is on the face uv the waters. The waves is a rollin mountin high, the litenin flashes ominous thro the gloom, and the deep-mouthed thunder mutters angrily in the distants. Ez a sentinel on the watch-tower, I look out, and what do I see? I see the old ship uv State loaded down with a valuable cargo uv Post-offices, Collectorships, and sich, a laborin in the trough uv the sea, her bowsprit cove in, her top-gallant lanyards bustid, her jib-boom a flutterin in the gale, her capstan spliced, and her sheet anker torn to ribbons. (Not hevin bin a sailor, only ez a driver on the Wabash Kanal, it is possible my nautikle terms may not be altogether correct. But it makes no difference in the

interior uv Kentucky.) She is strivin to make her
harbor, and is workin manfully. Close behind her
is the long, low, rakish skooner Dimocrisy, with all
sale set, a tryin her best to overtake her and board
her. For a time it seemed ez tho she wood be successful, but alas! she is fallin astern, and every minnit the distance between em is a widenin, widenin,
widenin, and at present writin there ain't the re-
motest prospect uv their gettin within hailin distance
uv each other.

To drop mettafor (wich, by the way, I kin jerk
when I feel so disposed), the prospect isn't ez encouragin ez it wuz, and I fear, in fact I feel certain,
that the short cut to offis wich the Democrisy thought
it had found through Androo Johnson's veto, is reely
the longest way round. I cannot understand what
indoost the Dimocratic leaders, our chosin standard-
bearers, to make sich egrejus asses uv theirselves ez
to place enny dependence on Johnson at all. What
cood they hev bin thinkin uv? Wuz not our experience in 1864 sufficient to deter em from makin any
experiment wich involved abandonment uv any uv
our principles? Didn't we, in the hope uv ketchin
Abolition war votes, nominate MickLellan, and
didn't the war men jeer us, and flout us, and say,
" Behold, we hev better war men uv our own; why

shood we leave home to find that uv wich we hev a
plenty?" When Androo Johnson, in a fit uv temporary indignashun, split on Sumner, why did our
people, like idiots, pick him up, and endorse him
without givin the matter matoor considerashun —
without waitin for the fax? Didn't they know that
Sumner wuz a sort uv a dose uv calomel, wich
worked on the President's liver, and necessitated
the discharge uv all the offensive matter wich hed
accumulated doorin his long term uv Dimocrisy?
Uv course it wuz, and to-day Androo Johnson,
hevin in that speech got rid uv the last vestidge uv
Dimocrisy wich infected him, comes up a stronger
man agin us than ever. We made two errors: On
the 4th uv March, 1865, at his inoggerashun, when
he made a spectacle uv hisself, we murmured gently
to ourselves, "It's all right! he's yet wun uv us."
And we sed the same after the splurge uv the 22d
uv February last. Oh, my friends, they wuz both
fatal errors. Them spasms wuz the efforts uv a
noble nacher a tryin to git rid uv Locofocoism, and
from the fact that he immejitely after commenst a
missellaneously apintin Abilishnists and Republicans to offises, and hezn't showed a sine uv a disposition to extend his hand to a single confidin Democrat, it's my opinion he's succeeded.

We bet too heavy on the fight atween the President and Sumner. Sumner is ordained to alluz hev a gong uv sum kind, which he is also ordained to keep perpetually a poundin. He's bin for several years amusin hisself a poundin the Dimocrisy, and when there wuzn't enuff uv that to make it interestin, he turned on Johnson, and he'll pound at him till suthin else excites his wrath. He's a Spanish bull, possessin sharp horns, and a immense amount uv strength and agility, which he is continooally a wastin by jumpin at sich red flags ez are mischeevusly waved afore him. He's jest ez apt to gore his frends ez his enemies, and his lungin at Johnson wuz no sign that Johnson had gone back on Ablishnism.

But enuff uv this. Sence it hez become a fixed fact that the boorish tailor, who now by accident okkepies the place uv the marter Linkin, made vacant by his untimely death by the hand uv a vile assassin (whose only redeemin trait wuz that he wuz a stanch, uncompromisin Dimocrat), — now, I say, that it's plain that this drunken sot ain't agoin to distribute the patronage amongst us who need it so much, I ask, in indignashun, wat is it that we are asked to endorse?

He proposes to continue the Freedmen's Buro bizness.

He refooses to withdraw the military from the Dimokratic States.

He refooses to restore to our sufferin brethren uv the Dimocratic States the habis corpusses wich the tyrant Linkin wrested from them.

He keeps Jefferson Davis a pinin in a loathsome dungeon, and only refooses to bring him to trial becoz, 4sooth, he haint yet got things in the right shape to hang him.

I cood enumerate other insults and opressions he hez piled upon Dimocrats, but I forbear. I might, if I wuz disposed to harrow up the Dimocratic sole and lasserate the Dimocratic bosom, state how I wuz treated, when, on the 24th uv Febrooary last I made a delegashun uv myself, and went to Washington for the purpose uv layin before him the necessity uv the removal uv the postmaster at the Corners, and the apintment uv myself in his stead. I found that his speech had reached all other parts uv the Yoonited States ez soon ez it hed Kentucky, for there wuz suthin over a hundred thousand stanch Dimocrats there, all with petitions noomerously signed, wich they hed held over from Bookannon's administration, recommendin uv em to places. How wuz we reseeved? How did Androo Johnson treet us? I mite say how emphatically I wuz shoved out uv his room, and with what reckless profanity I heerd him remark that Washington had stunk with secesh ever since he vetoed the bill; that that foolish speech had acted on the whole country like a puke, and that each State had spewed its foulest material onto Washington, and that the atmosphere wuz heavy with their breath, et settry, et settry, but I forbear.

Suffice it to say that the few Democratic members uv Congress had hard work borrowin money enuff to git the most spectable uv the crowd home agin, and even then thousands uv em who wuz drawed there by that speech, shoor uv apintments, wuz obliged to *walk* home ignominiously, uv whom I wuz which.

Androo Johnson may be worthy uv Dimocratic support, but he hez a queer way uv showin it. I know not wat others may do, but ez for me and my household I'll run after no strange gods. Ef he wants us, let him call on us in language wich we kin understand.

Petroleum V. Nasby,

Lait Paster uv the Church uv the Noo Dispensashun.

7

XV.

*The Patriarchal System. — An Affecting Appeal
in Behalf of a Friend.*

CONFEDERIT X ROADS
(wich is in the Stait uv Kentucky),
March 19, 1866.

YESTERDAY I happened to pick up a kopy
uv a friteful depraved Ablishin paper, and my
horror-stricken eyes wuz glued to the follerin passage, which I read : —

" I am happy to state to you that our free negroes
are doing finely. We have no trouble with them.
They have all gone to work manfully. They give
an impetus to trade that we never before had. I
have sold John Guttle's negroes, this year and last,
more goods than I ever sold Guttle, and he owned
two hundred and fifty slaves. So you see the free
negro system is working well with us."

Ez I peroozed them lines, tears started involun-
tarily from my beamin eyes, and coursed in torrents
down my venerable cheeks. I know John Guttle

well, I may say intimately. He wuz a dear friend,
— one uv the few wich I kall friend in the most
catholic and comprehensive sense uv the word. He
holds my note fur eighteen dollars and 63 cents ; and
I hev sumwhere among my papers, wich I have
alluz carefully preserved for reference, a memorandum uv his address, that I might be shoor not to
forget to send it to him. I give him the note becoz
he furnished the paper, and it made him easy in his
mind — I put down the memorandum bekoz it
looked business-like. Benevolence is a prominent
trait in my karacter. When givin my note for
borrered money will do a man good, I never be-
grudge the trouble uv writin it.

But wat I wuz a goin to say wuz, that the feend-
ishnis uv that item passes belief. The writer puts
it in print to show that the Ablishn uv slavry benefitted sumbody. I grant him that the merchant,
who undoubtedly wuz born in Massachusetts, wuz
benefitted by the change ; so are the greesy mechanics who are now pollutin the soil uv Alabama ; and
so, probably, are the 250 niggers ; but, in the name
uv Liberty, in the name uv Justice, in the name uv
the Constertooshun uv the Yoonited States, and the
flag uv our Common Country, I ask, How about
John Guttle?

John Guttle is robbed. John Guttle is deprived uv his property. The bred is taken from John Guttle's mouth ; his staff is broken ; his dependence is gone ; he is bereft.

Never shall I forget John Guttle or his hospitable mansion, ez I knowed it in the happy year afore the crooel war. He wuz a gentleman uv the old skool — one uv the few left us in these degenerate days. His home wuz wun uv unalloyed happiness. Situated just back uv Mobeel, he had the finest plantashun in that section, and hed on it 250 niggers. All shades wuz represented. There wuz the coal-black Cuffee, whose feechers denoted the pure Afrikin, and whose awkward manners showed that he wuz not long from Afrika. There wuz the civilized mulatto, in whose veins the Guttle blood showed ; the quadroon, in whom the good old Guttle blood predominated ; and the octoroon, which wuz mostly Guttle. The Guttleses wuz eminently a Christian generation. They wuz devoutly pious ; and there never wuz one uv the name who cood not repeat, without the book, all uv the texts bearin on slavery. The passages in which Onesimus and Hager figger wuz favorites with em ; but on " cussid be Canaan " they wuz strong. For generations they had mourned over the hard fate uv the sons uv Ham, doomed to

perpetooal bondage becoz uv the sin uv their father;
and with a missionary spirit ekaled by few and ex-
celled by none, they did their part towards redoosin
that cuss, by makin ez many of em ez possible half-
bruthers to the more favored race uv Japhet, and
thus bringing uv em out uv the cuss; and they had
mellered the color uv their charges down from the
hideous black to a bright yeller. Under the old
patriarkle system, time passed orf smoothly and
pleasantly with the Guttle family. Them 250 niggers wuz obliged, uv course, to work, and their labor wuz money. John bought each uv the male
sons uv Ham too soots uv close per annum, and
each uv the female sons uv Ham one soot. It wuz
considered healthy for the young ones to go naked,
which they wuz religiously allowed to do, ez none
uv the Guttles uv that family wood do any thing
agin nater or her laws. The girls hed pianos, and
wuz educated at the North; the boys wuz celebrat-
ed for horse racing and their skill at losin money at
faro. They wuz hospitable and generous to a fault.
Their house wuz open house, and their beverages
wuz alluz the best. Money wuz no objick to them;
for when they had a severe attack of poker, or faro,
or hoss racin, they hed plenty uv octoroons and
quadroons, with the real Guttle nose, wich brand

wuz well known in Noo Orleans, and wood alluz command the highest possible figger that wuz paid in that market; or, ef they had no more than they wanted at home uv that style, why, a few field hands wood be sold, and the remainin ones wood be persuaded by the overseer to do the work uv the whole. John Guttle's sons wuz all in the Confederit army. His daughters, willin to sacrifice every thing fur the cause, heroically pledged theirselves to whip the niggers theirselves doorin their absence.

Now all is changed! A shadder hez fallen across that peaceful home. The nigger quarters is there, but the niggers is not. The broad plantashun is divided up into small farms, and half uv it is owned by Ablishnists from the North, who work theirselves, and who hev a meetin house on one corner uv it, and the niggers a skool house on the tother. The race track is plowed up and in cotton; the whippin-post and the stocks is taken down and burned; all, all the evidences uv civilizashun hez faded afore the ruthless hand of the invader. John Guttle — that generous old man — subsists by the labor uv his own hands. One uv his sons ekes out a miserable existence running a dray in Mobeel; another, who is gifted with no ordinary intelleck, earns a respectable livin playin seven-up, in a small way, with his former niggers; and the two girls is runnin a sewing masheen.

Talk not to me uv benefits. What is a dozen tradesmen and two hundred and fifty niggers to the gellorious old Dimocratic John Guttle? What is the interest uv a dozen or so uv Noo England mechanics, and the niggers aforesaid, when compared to that glorious aristocracy which can never exist beside em? Kin I go and borrer eighteen dollars and sixty-three cents uv one uv them? No. Becoz, working for their paltry livins, they place a higher valyoo on money, and will not spread it around ez profoosely ez the noble race which preceded em.

Another great wrong is done in this settin free uv John Guttle's niggers. John Guttle hez, uv course, no further interest in the Dimocratic party. Slavery wuz the umbillikle cord which united the Southern slaveholder and the Northern Dimocrat; and, that cord cut, why hez John Guttle any more interest in Dimocracy? We stood ez a Chinese wall between them and the rushin flood uv Ablishn fanaticism; and we made the wall biznis pay. They furnished money, and we did the work; and, there bein but few uv us, the orfisis wuz easily divided. Alas! our okepashin's gone. The South is forever lost to us; for she has no dirty work for us to do.

I appeal to the Yoonited States uv America.   In behalf uv John Guttle, I say, give him back his niggers.   In behalf uv the Dimocrisy North who are out uv employment, give him back his niggers. In behalf uv his son who is runnin a dray, give him back his niggers.   In behalf uv his daughters runnin a sewin machine, give him back his niggers.   Make things Normal agin.   Like John the Baptist, the Government shall hear the voice uv one howlin in the wilderness until all these is done.

PETROLEUM V. NASBY,
Lait Paster uv the Church uv the Noo Dispensashun.

XVI.

A Dream. — The Corpse of Republicanism. — Who the Mourners were, and how they felt. — The awakening of the Sleeping Giant, and the Scattering that followed.

CONFEDRIT × ROADS
(wich is in the Stait uv Kentucky),
March 30, 1866.

I HEV bin to Washinton. That Ablishn Postmaster at the Corners hed become to me a nitemare. Day after day I seed him a handlin guvment money, drawin his salery promptly, and takin his drinks reglerly, while I, a Constooshnel Dimekrat, a supporter uv our great and good President, wuz forced to the humiliashun uv waitin till I wuz treated, ceptin when a new grocery keeper cum in, which gave me a chance to establish a credit for a short time. I felt that sumthin must be done, and therefore I went to Washinton.

Knowin that for men uv my profound convickshins, holdin my views ez to consiliashen and sich,

I hed no call to go to the Postmaster-General, who is a Ablishnist, I went dreckly to the Second Jaxon hisself. I succeeded in gettin a audience late in the afternoon. Our patron saint wuz a sittin at a table, eggsausted with receevin delegashens and sich.

"Well," sed he.

"Honerd and spected sir," said I, "I am a applicant for the post orfis at Confedrit X Roads, wich is at present held by a Ablishnist who does not beleeve in yoor policy, wich I do beleeve in solemnly. Spected and honered sir," sed I, "ef I shood have twins born to me this nite, I shood name em both Policy."

"Wich State are yoo from?" sed he, half asleep.

"From Kentucky, honered and spected sir," sed I.

"Well," sed he, yawnin feerfully, and turnin to a clerk, "FILL OUT A PARDON, AND GIVE HIM A COMMISSION!"

"Honered and spected sir," sed I, in a fit of loonacy for wich I can't account, "I don't need a pardon. I wuz never in the late lamented Confedrit servis."

"What'n thunder, then, are yoo here for, beggin a post offis? Git out, yoo imposter!" and I wuz too wunst ignominiously showed to the door. I didn't quite understand the lay uv the land around the White House.

In vane I tried to git back, that I might convince him I did ez much for the Confederasy ez my humble abilities permitted, and that I needed consiliatin ez badly ez anybody. Then, hart broke and dead broke, not heving the wherewith to prokoor more sootable lodgin, I lay me down on the cold stun steps, and sought refuge from my troubles in sleep.

I dreemed a dream. Methawt I wuz in a room in the White House. Stretched out on one side uv the room wuz the corpse uv a giant, a monster in size and strength, but withal uv a pleasin presence, and fair to look upon. Onto its head was a liberty cap, and by its side wuz a sword, considerably dinted, and with all the gildin knocked off.

"Wat is these?" sed I, pointin to the corpse, askin a sort uv a attendant.

"Them," replied he, "is the defunct carcass uv Republikinism. He was a hefty yooth in his day, but he died this mornin. Look! the mourners are a comin to divide his clothes."

And shoor enuff, they came in. At the head wuz the second Jaxon, which the Ablishnists derisively call Moses, who appeared to be angry, and clost behind him wuz Seward, a weepin out uv one eye,

and a smilin out uv tother, and Jim Lane, who hed
a handkercher wich he occasionally put to his eyes,
but wich I notist wuz ez dry ez a lime kiln, and
Doolittle, and Lee, and Raymond, and Beauregard,
and Cowan, and Stephens, and Thurlow Weed, and
Vallandigham, and Governor Sharkey, and a host uv
others, all uv wich ranged theirselves around the bier.

"He wuz a promisin yooth," sed Seward, a puttin his handkercher to his eyes, "but the atmosphere
uv the White House wuz too much for him. I
insist, however," sed he, a pocketin the handkercher, and takin hold uv a trinket the corpse held in
his hand, labelled "Presidency, 1868," from which
hung mor'n a million uv smaller trinkets, "that ez
'twas me that pizened him, this is mine."

"Nary," sed Johnson; "I did the biziness for
him, and it's mine."

"Settle it ez yoo please," sed Raymond, gently,
"but whoever gits it must remember that this Secretaryship is mine."

"And I," sed Doolittle, "must hev, for my assistance, this little affair marked 'St. James,' for my
seat in the Senit is a goner."

"For my part," sed Jim Lane, "the western appointments is mine. Its worth em all to wear this
collar."

"My friends," sed Stephens, "I find no amnesty about the corpse. There must be one manufactured and stuck in his pocket, to be prodoost at the funeral."

Thurlow Weed sed nothin, but looked on with a sardonic smile, knowin perfeckly well that whoever took the biggest part uv the plunder, he'd control it, any way.

Governor Sharkey laid claim to a secretaryship, and Boregard to the place uv Sherman, and Lee to Grant's position, and Vallandigham wanted this, and tother feller that, and there wuz a terrible hubbub over the corpse. Wilkes Booth's gost came in, and wanted to know what he wuz to hev in the new deal, "for," sed he, "ef't hadn't bin for me, where'd yoo all hev bin? Talk uv the White House atmosphere killin him! I'm sure the shadder uv the buildin blasted what little uv his spirit yoo hed," sed he, a turnin to Seward, "but ef Linkin hed lived, ha, ha!" sed he, in a tragedy voise. Then in trooped a lot uv other gosts. There wuz Bill Allen, uv Ohio, and Washington Hunt, uv Noo York, and Jeems Bookannon, uv Pennsylvania, and Eli Thayer, and Lew. Campbell, and Garret Davis, who started to make a speech, but the entire assemblage stuck their fingers in their ears, wich hint he took for the first time in his life, and desisted.

Finally Johnson swore " by the eternal" (he got that noshun from the first A. J., wich he thinks he resembles, coz his innitials is the same, and coz the original vetoed a bill wunst) that he wood hev the Presidency, and gobbled it. Seward, he snatched at it, and they tussled. The company stood by to see it out, for it made but little difference to them wich got it. In the skrimage Johnson happened to ram Seward up agin a window on the north side uv the room, and smashed it out. Jest then a blast uv north wind poured into the room through the aperture, and blowed onto the face uv the corpse. The effect was electrikle. Life ran through his veins, his face flushed, and the livid hue was changed to the ruddy glow uv health. The dead wuz alive; the giant raised to his feet, and looked around him, shakin off them ez wuz a hangin to him like insex. Noticin the trinket wich hed caused the skrimage in Johnson's hand, he took him by the neck, and twistin it out uv his hand, flung him gently through the winder. " I ain't made up my mind who to give this to, but yoo bet it ain't yoo," sed he.

" Willyum," sed he, turnin to Seward, "I'm surprised at yoo. Wuz this bauble the price uv yoor honesty and yoor principle? Go, Willyum! Ez for yoo, Doolittle, yoo never wuz half baked; yoo,

Thurlow, put Raymond in your vest pocket, and quit the presence. Yoo, Jim Lane, I leave to the tender mercies uv my friends in Kansas. Clear out the balance uv this rabble, and send for my friends. I've bin pizened, and smothered, and stunk nigh to death. Clear out the house, and sweep it, and sprinkle chloride uv lime, and sich, all over it. Shut down them Southern windows, and open those on the North, East, and West sides. I want a snuff uv fresh air, for I — "

At this pint I awoke, and found myself, not in the White House, but on the steps thereof, cold and shiverin. In my pocket wuz the papers wich didn't get me the post orifis I wuz seekin, and in my mind wuz chaotic confusion. Wuz the dream prophetic, or wuz it merely a vagary uv the mind, wich, wen loosed from its clay, sores off onto its own hook, without any restraint. Is the giant Republican actually dead, or is he in a trance? Will it arise, and scatter them ez hez appinted themselves administrators uv its estate, and wich are beginnin to divide the assets, or will he stay ded? Wood, oh wood, that I knowed!

PETROLEUM V. NASBY.

Lait Paster uv the Church of the New Dispensashun.

XVII.

A Kentucky Tea Party. — Opinion entertained by
Mrs. Deacon Pogram of Charles Sumner. —
Discussion between Mrs. Deacon P. and an
Illinois Store-keeper of the name of Pollock. —
Miscegenation.

CONFEDRIT × ROADS ⎫
(wich is in the Stait uv Kentucky), ⎬
April 1, 1866. ⎭

CHARLES SUMNER is not a very popular
man in this section uv Kentucky; on the
contrary, quite the reverse. He is known here ez
an Ablishnist; ez one who is a chief supporter uv
that hidjus sin — the infidelity, I may say, for a
man may ez well deny the whole Bible ez to cast
discredit upon Onesimus, Hagar, and Ham, onto
wich the whole system uv Afrikin slavery rests —
the origenator, therefore, uv the infidle beleef that
Slavery is not uv divine origin, wich, judjin from
the experience uv the last five years, appears to be
gainin ground in the North. He is not, therefore,
popular in this region.

Yisterday I attendid a tea party at Deekin Pogram's, to wich the elite uv the Corners wuz present, incloodin an Illinoy store-keeper uv the name uv Pollock, wich hed bin invited because the Deekin hed, some three months ago, bought a bill uv goods uv him on ninety days' time, and wantid an extension.

While at the table enjoyin the

"Cup wich cheers, but don't intoxicate very much,"

ez Dryden hez it, tho I bleeve, to keep off chills, in this country, they mix three and a half parts uv whiskey to one uv tea, the name uv Sumner wuz mentioned.

Mrs. Pogram to-wunst remarked that she didn't want the name uv that ojus creecher spoken at her table.

"Why?" sed I, gratified at the ebulition.

"I hate him!" sed she, spitefully.

"So do I," replied I; "but what hev yoo agin him, aside from his obnoxious political opinions?"

"Didn't he marry a nigger?" sed Mrs. P., triumphantly. "Didn't he marry a nigger — a full-blooded nigger? and hezn't he hed nineteen yaller children, every one uv wich he compelled, agin their will, to marry full-blooded niggers? Didn't he — "

8

" Mrs. P.," sed this Illinoy store-keeper, wich his
name it wuz Pollock, " do yoo object to miscegenation?"

" Missee— what?" replied she, struck all uv a
heap at the word.

"Miscegenation — amalgamation — marryin whites
with niggers."

" Do I?" retorted she; "ketch a son uv mine
marryin a nigger! They are another race; they'r
beasts; and who'd marry em but jist sich men ez
Sumner and them other Ablishnists?"

" Then permit me to ask," sed this Pollock, wich
wuz bound to kick up a muss, " ef ther's any race
uv pure blood in this section uv Kentucky, wich is
yaller?"

" No! uv course not," sed Mrs. P.; " them yaller
people is mulatters — half nigger, half white."

" And them ez is quite white — not quite, but
nearly so — about the color uv a new saddle, like
Jane, there," sed he, pintin to a octoroon girl uv 18
wich used to belong to the Deekin afore the isshooin
uv the infernal proclamashen, " like Jane, there,
wich is waitin on the Deekin, and — but, good
Lord!" sed he, startin up like a tragedian.

" Wat!" shouted the company, all startin up.

" Nothin," sed he: " only, now that Jane's face is

in range with the Deekin's, wat a wonderful resemblance! She hez the Pogram nose and ginral outline uv face; not Mrs. P.'s angularity, but the Deekin all over. My deer sir," sed he, addressin the Deekin, " ef she wuzn't a quadroon, I shood say she looks enough like yoo to be yoor daughter, by a first wife, I shood say, for she hez not, ez I remarked, Mrs. P.'s angularity and gineral boneinis; but uv course, she bein a part nigger, the resemblance may be sat down ez-a-very-remarkable-coincidence!"

The Deekin turned ez white ez a sheet, and Mrs. Pogram turned ez red ez a biled lobster, from wich I inferred that there wuz trooth in a rumor I had heerd about the Deekin and his wife hevin a misunderstandin about a nigger woman and her baby, about 18 years ago, wich resulted in his bein made bald-headed in less than a minute, and the baby's mother being sold South. The Illinoy store-keeper, uv the name uv Pollock, resoomed, —

" I wuz about askin wat them niggers is ez is nearly white?"

" Why, they'r octoroons, or seven-eighths white," sed Mrs. Pogram.

" And no Kentuckian ever marries a nigger?" inquired the store-keeper, who I saw wuz pursooin his investigations altogether too fur.

"Never!" sed Mrs. Pogram; "we leave that to Ablishnists."

"Well, then," sed this Pollock, who, I spect, wuzn't half so innsent ez he let on, "I see that yoo hev no objection to mixin with the nigger, providin yoo don't do it legally; that amalgamashen don't hurt nothin, pervidin yoo temper it with adultery. Is that the idee, Mrs. Pogram?"

Mrs. P. wuz mad, and made no reply, and Pollock persood the subjick.

"Jane there, is, I take it, about one-eighth nigger. She got her white blood from whites, uv course; and ez there coodent be no marryin in the biznis, there is proof positive in her face that the 8th commandment hez bin violated about four times somewhere in this vicinity, or wherever her maternal ancestors, on her mother's side, may hev resided. What do yoo think about it, Deekin? Ez a Christian, woodent it be better to marry em than to add a violation uv the commandment to the sin uv amalgamashen? It wood redoose yoor load jest a half."

The Deekin wuz too indignant to reply, and ez it involved a pint altogether too hefty for his limited intelleck, I took it up.

"My dear sir," I remarked, "yoo don't make the proper distinction, or, rather, yoo don't appreciate the subjick at all. The nigger here sustains only one character with us, — that uv a inferior bein, the slave uv the hawty Caucashen, uv whom we are the noblest specimens; that is, the Deekin is, he bein a Southerner. I unfortunately wuz born in the North, and am a hawty Caucashen only by adoption. To marry a nigger wood be to destroy our idea uv sooperiority, for we marry only our ekals. The intercourse with em, the results uv wich yoo see indications, bein outside uv the pale uv matrimony, is not, ez yoo wood suppose, the result uv unbrideled licentiousnis, but is merely the assertion uv our superiority. When the lordly Caucashen (uv whom the Deekin is wich) bids a daughter uv Ham (wich, in the orginal Hebrew, signifies the hindquarter uv a hog) come to him, and she doth it not, he breaks her head, wich inculcates obedience. One is only a slave indeed when he surrenders all his individyooel rites. The female slave cannot be considered ez entirely subdooed until she hez yielded to her owner everything. To marry em wood be to elevate em; the intercourse common among us is not a sin, it bein merely the assertion uv that superiority wich we claim is founded on the Holy Scripter. See Onesimus, Hagar, and Ham."

"Yes," sed the Deekin, who wuz now on the

right track; " it's a assertion uv our sooperiority;
it's a dooty every white man owes to his class, and
I, for one, will alluz — "

" Let me ketch yoo at it, Gabe Pogram," shouted
Mrs. P., " and I'll give you sich a cat-haulin ez yoo
never — drat yoor sooperiority, and yoor Ham, and
yoor Caucashen. Niggers is niggers, and — "

Noticin that Mrs. Pogram hedn't quite arrived at
the proper pitch uv self-sacrifice, I turned the discussion onto Sumner agin, ez a subjick upon wich
they cood all agree.

I learned that his father wuz a Dutch grocery-
keeper, and his mother an Irish washer-woman;
that he run away from home at the tender age of 8,
after murderin, in cold blood, his grandparents, one
uv wich wuz a Jew and tother a Chinese; that he
wuz apprenticed to the shoemakin biznis, and hed
cut the throat uv his boss and his wife, and im-
mersed the younger children into a biler uv scaldin
water, where they were found mostly dead seven
hours afterward; that he acquired wealth a sellin
lottry tickets and brass clocks, et settry. His servants wuz redoost Southern gentlemen wich he hed
swindled into his debt, and wich, under the laws uv
Massychoosits, coodent git away, and that his inti-
mate friends and associates wuz niggers, with wich

he sot long at the festive board, and drunk cham-
pane; that Lucresha Mott wuz his sister, Anna
Dickinson his daughter, Fred Douglas his half-
brother, and that he kissed, habitually, every nigger
child he met, and frowned so severially onto white
children ez to throw em into spasms, and other
items uv information uv wich, livin in the North, I
wuz ignorant. Ez I remarked, he isn't popular
down here, and cood hardly be elected to Congris
from this Deestrick. The tea party broke up shortly
after, Pollock winkin at me villainously ez he left
the house, feelin good to think how he hed opened
a old sore. That Pollock needs watchin.

PETROLEUM V. NASBY,
Lait Paster uv the Church uv the Noo Dispensashun.

XVIII.

A Cry of Exultation. — A Gleam of Light.

CONFEDRIT X ROADS
(wich is in the Stait uv Kentucky),
April 2, 1866.

KIN it be? Is it troo, or is it not troo? Is Androo Johnson all my fancy painted him, or is he still a heaven-defying persekooter uv the Democratic Saints? That's wat I and some thousands uv waitin souls wood go suthin handsome to know.

I confess I never quite lost faith in Androo.

Pro-slavery Democracy sticks to a man ez does the odor uv the gentle skunk to clothes, and it is got rid uv only by the same means, to-wit, buryin the victim thereof.

Androo started out to be a Moses, and he is one; but I think he's changed his Israelites. I onst saw a woman skinnin live eels, and I reproached her, saying, —

"Woman, why skinnest thou eels alive? Doth it not pain em?"

"Nary!" retorted she. "I've skinned em this way for going on to 20 years, and they're used to it."

Even so. The negroes hev bin in bondage so long that they're used to it, and Androo feelin a call to continue in the Moses biznes, hez, I hope, turned his attention to the Dimocrisy. It's us he's a-goin to lead up out uv the Egypt uv wretchedness we've bin in for neerly five years; it's us that's a-goin to quit brick making without straw, and go up into the Canaan wich is runnin with the milk and honey uv public patronage. We shel hev sum fites: there's Amakelitish post masters and Phillistine collectors to displace, but with a second Jaxon at our hed what can we fear?

I feel to-night like a young colt. To me it seems ez though my venerable locks, wich hangs scantily about my temples, hed grown black agin, and that my youth was returnin. Ef I hed any notion uv sooiside, them idea is dismist. I'm young agin. Wat hez worked this change? you ask. It's the proclamation declarin the war at an end, and withdrawin from the Dimocratic States the odious hirelins uv the tyrant Linkin, and the doin away uv that terrible marshal law. That's wat's done it for me.

Now I feel like sayin, with one uv old, "Mine eyes hev seed thy glory; let thy servant depart in peace."

We hev bin dooly subjoogated some time, and a waitin for this. We wantid it, and longed for it ez the hart does for the water course, and considerably more, onless the hart wuz thirsty in the extreme. For now we are in the Yoonyun agin; we are under the shadder uv that glorious old flag wich protects all men ceptin niggers and ablishnists. The nigger is left to be adjustid by us, who is to be governed by the laws wich control labor and capital. Certenly he is — uv coarse. I saw two uv my neighbors adjustin one last nite. They wuz doin it with a paddle, wich wuz bored full uv holes. He didn't seem to enjoy it ez much ez they did. By that proclamation our states are agin under their own control. Let em go at wunst to work to destroy all the vestiges uv the crooel war through wich they hev past. There aint no solgers now to interfere, for the policy uv keepin soldiers in and among free people is abhorrent to freedom and humanity. Go to work at wunst, and build up the broken walls uv your Zion.

We must hev Peace and unanimity; and Peace cannot dwell among us onless there's a oneness uv purpose and sentiment. To prokoor this is yoor fust dooty. If there be among you them ez opposed

yoo doorin yoor late struggle for Rites, hist em.
Their presence is irritatin, and kin not be tolerated.
Ablishunism is as abhorrent now as ever, and the
sooner yoo are rid uv it the better. It is safe to
assume that every man who opposed the lately
deceased confederacy is a Ablishnist.

The next step, and the most important, is to tear
down the nigger school houses and churches wich
hev bin built here and there, and kindly take the
nigger by the ear, and lead him back to his old
quarters, wich is his normal position. The Yankee
school teachers sent here by Freedmen's Aid Socie-
ties shood properly be hung for spreadin dissatisfac-
tion and spellin books among the niggers, but I
wood advise mercy and consiliation. Tar and
featherin, with whippins, will perhaps do ez well,
and will go to show the world that our justice is
tempered with charity ; that we kin be generous ez
well ez just. Yoor Legislatures shood be instantly
called together, and proper laws for the government
uv the Freedmen should be passed. Slavery is
abolisht, and the people must live up to the require-
ments of the act in good faith. I protest agin any
violation uv good faith, but labor must be done, for
the skripter commands it, and our frail nature demands wat cant be got without it. We don't like

to do it, but shel skripter be violated? Not at all.
The nigger must do it hisself, not ez a slave, for
slavery is abolished, but ez a free man.   Ethiopean
citizens uv Amerikin descent (wich is mulatters),
and full-blooded blacks, and all hevin in the veins
a taint uv Afrikin blood, must be restrained gently,
and for their own good, I suggest laws ez follows : —

1. They must never leave the plantation onto
wich they are, when this act goes into effect, without
a pass from the employer, under penalty uv bein
shot.

2. They shel hev the privilege uv suein every-
body uv their own color, ef they kin give white bail
for costs.

3. They shel hev the full privilege uv bein sued
the same ez white folks.

4. They shel be competent ez witnesses in cases
in wich they are not interested, but their testimony
is to go for nothin ef it is opposed by the testimony
uv a white man or another nigger.

5. No nigger shel be allowed to buy or lease real
estate outside uv any incorporated city, town, or
village.

6. No nigger shel be allowed to buy or lease real

estate within any incorporated city, town, or village, except as hereinafter provided for, to wit: —

He shel give notice uv his desires by publication for six consecutive weeks in some noosepaper uv general circulation in sed village, for wich publication he shel pay invariably in advance. He shel then give bonds, in sich sums ez the mayor shel decide, that neither he, nor any uv his ancestors, or descendants, or relations, will ever become public charges, and will always behave themselves with doo humility, the bondsmen to be white men and freeholders. Then the mayor shel cause a election to be proclaimed, and if the free white citizens shel vote "yea" unanimously, he shel be allowed to buy or lease real estate. If there is a dissenting vote, then he shel be put onto the chain gang for six months for his impudence in makin sich a request.

7. Their wages shel be sich ez they and the employers shel mutually agree; but that the negroes may not become luxurious and effeminate, wich two things is vices wich goes to sap the simplicity and strength uv a people, the sum shel never exceed $5 per month, but not less than enuff in all cases to buy him one soot uv close per annum, wich the employer shel purchase hisself.

8. The master shell hev the privilege uv addin to

this code sich other rules and regulations for their proper government ez may strike him ez being good for em from time to time.

These provisions sekure the nigger in all the rites wich kin reasonably be asked for him, just elevated ez he is from slavery, and thrown upon the world, ignorant of the dooties of his new position and status. He is simple, and needs the guidin hand uv the stronger race.

My hart is too full to make further suggestions. Organized into a tabloo, with the constitooshun in one hand (wich beloved instrument kivers a great deal of ground), a scar-bangled spanner in the other, and a tramplin on a bloo coat wich I stript orf uv a returned nigger solger wich wuz sick, I exultinly exclaim, "The Union ez it is is ez good ez the Union ez it wuz. 'Ror!"

PETROLEUM V. NASBY,
Lait Paster uv the Church uv the Noo Dispensashun.

XIX.

A Wail of Anguish. — The Passage of the Civil Rights Bill over the Veto.

CONFEDRIT X ROADS
(wich is in the Stait uv Kentucky),
April 9, 1866.

I AM a kittle full of cusses.

Under me is a burnin fire uv rage, wich is bein continyooally fed with the oil uv disappointment.

And I bile over.

The civil rites bill, wich our Moses put his foot into, we thought wuz dead.

And we fired great guns, and hung out our flags, wich we laid aside in 1860, and made a joyful noise.

For we said, one unto another, Lo! he is a true Moses, inasmuch ez he is a leadin us out uv the wilderness.

The civil rites bill wuz the serpent wat bit us, and he histed it, that we might look and live.

Now let us be joyful !

For the Ethiopian is delivered into our hands,
bound hand and foot.

Blessed be Moses !

We will make him grind our corn ; but he shel
not eat thereof.

Blessed be Moses !

We will make him tread out our wheat ; but we
will muzzle his mouth.

Blessed be Moses !

He shall pick our cotton ; but the hire he receiv-
eth, he shall stick in his eye without injuring the
sight thereof.

Blessed be Moses !

He shall toil in the sugar mill ; but the sugar
shall he not sell.

Blessed be Moses !

His sweat shall nourish our corn ; but he shall
eat nary ear thereof.

Blessed be Moses !

We will burn his school houses, and destroy his
spelling books (for shall the nigger be our superior?), and who shall stay our hand?

The skool teachers we will tar and feather, and
whar is the bloo-koted hirelins to make us afeerd?

Blessed be Moses !

We looked at the nigger, and said, Ha, ha! the last state uv that chattle is wuss nor the fust; for before, we hed his labor while he wuz strong and healthy, but hed to take care on him when he wuz sick and old; and now we kin git his labor without the care.

Blessed be Moses!

The Ablishnists cast out one devil, and garnished the room; but there wuz seven devils more stronger and hungrier, which rushed in and pre-empted the premises.

Blessed be Moses!

But our song uv joy wuz turned into a wale uv anguish.

Moses sought to hist the serpent, but the serpent histed him.

He's on a pole, and the bitin North wind is a blowin onto him.

He can't get up any higher, because his pole ain't any longer; and he cant't get down, because he ain't no place to light onto.

He vetoed the bills, and Congress hez vetoed him; the civil rights bill they passed in a uncivil manner.

Now, bein the nigger hez rights, he is our ekal.

Our ekil is the nigger now, and onless the skool

9

house is burned, and the spellin books destroyed, he
will soon be our superior.

We wuz willin to give him the right uv bein sued ;
but, alas ! he kin sue.

He kin be a witness agin us, and he kin set his
face agin ourn.

Our wise men may make laws to keep him in his
normal speer, but uv wat avail is they?

We kin buy and sell him no more, neither he nor
his children.

The men will cleave unto their wives, and the
wives unto their husbands, and our hand is powerlis
to separate em.

Their children kin we no more put up at auction,
and sell to the highest bidder, we pocketing joyfully
the price thereof.

They hev become sassy and impudent, and say,
" Go to ; are we not men?"

I bade one git orf the sidewalk, and he bade me
be damned.

I chucked a nearly white one under the chin, and
smiled onto her, and she squawked ; and her husband, hearin the squawk thereof, came up and bustid
my head, even as a white man wood hev dun.

I chastised wun who gave me lip ; and he sood

me, a Caucashun, for assault and battery, and got a judgment!

Wale! for Moses put out his hand to save us these indignities, but his hand wuz too weak.

We killed Linkin in vain.

Our Moses is playin Jaxon. He fancieth he resembleth him, becoz his inishals is the same.

He resembleth Jaxon muchly — in that Jaxon hed a policy wich he cood carry out, while our Moses hez a policy wich he can't carry out.

And ez he can't carry out his policy, the people are carryin it out for him.

Wich they do, a holdin it at arm's length, and holdin their noses.

Moses is a cake half baked; he is hot on one side, and cold on tother.

He darsn't let go uv Ablishnism, and is afeerd to come to us.

He hez been takin epsom salts and epecac; and one is workin up, and the other is workin down.

Where kin we look for comfort?

Do we turn to the people? Connecticut answers, " 'Ror for Hawley!" and Noo Hampshier goes Ablishun.

Do we turn to the courts? Lo! Taney hez gone to his reward — him who aforetime dealt out Dimekratic justice, and who understood the nacher uv the nigger, — and Chase, who is pizen, reigns in his stead.

Raymond is growin weak in the knees, and Doolittle is a broken reed on which to lean.

We are too short at both ends.

Shall we go to Brazil? Lo! there they put niggers in office.

Mexico holds out her hands to us; but, lo! the nigger is considered a man.

We hev no escape from the Etheopian; he is around us, and about us, and on top uv us.

I see no post orfis in the distance, no hope for the future.

Hed I been a Ablishunist, so ez to make the thing safe in the next world, I shood be glad to die, and quit this.

For my sole is pregnant with grief; my hart bugs out with woe.

PETROLEUM V. NASBY,
Lait Paster uv the Church uv the Noo Dispensashun.

XX.

Mournful View of the Situation.

CONFEDRIT X ROADS
(wich is in the Stait uv Kentucky),
April 26, 1866.

THE work uv death is a goin on. The sakred precepts uv the Holy Skripters is bein daily violated by an insane majority, who hev substitooted their own noshens for the safe and pleasant reve-lashens uv Holy Writ, and the practices of their fathers.

Cood Noah, when he cussed Ham, and declared that he shood be a servant unto his brethren, hev foreseen how his cuss wood hev bin disregarded in these degenerate days, he wood, I boldly assert (and I make the assertion from wat I know uv the char-acter uv that eminent navigator), hev kep sober, and not cusst Ham at all. For wat's the yoose uv sich a cuss ef it's to be removed jist when you want it to stick? Hed it bin taken off afore cotton wuz profit-able, and afore the Southern people hed learned to depend onto their labor, it wouldent hev bin so bad, and they cood hev endoored it without murmurin. But, alars! not only is the South in a state of abject cussitood, but the Northern Dimocrasy is likewise.

The case stood thuswise: The South depended on the Nigger; and the Northern politicians, like me, depended on the South. The nigger wuz the foundashun upon wich the entire structur rested; and now that he's knocked out, it falls.

I wuz in Washington the other day, and wuz a unwillin witnis uv a scene wich filled me with unutterable disgust. The niggers wuz a celebratin suthin connected with their onnatural removal from their normal condishun, and wuz a paradin the streets with bands uv music, and with banners and inscriptions. They hed the impudence to dress up in good clothes, — clothes wich I cood not afford to wear, — and three uv the impudent cusses hed the ashoorance to go so far in their imitation of human beins ez to make speeches; and to my horrer, the mass uv em hed ben so well trained by somebody that they actily cheered, and ez near ez I cood make out got in the applause at the right place, and all without the assistance uv a indivijjle to commence applaudin at the right time, wich we hev generally found nessary at Dimmekratic meetins.

Their inscripshuns wuz insultin. They hed em all spelt rite, and they wuz full uv aloosions to ekal rites, and onqualifyed suffrage, and sich, planely showin that the poor, misguided critters hed no idee that they wuz loaded down with a cuss, and that becoz uv that cuss they hed no rites watever.

In Richmond I saw other evidences uv the terrible breakin down uv the barriers wich Noah set up atween the races. I wuz sittin in a hoss car, when a nigger hed the onparalleled asshoorence to enter and set down. I remonstrated with the chattel, who laft in my face.

Thus the old landmarks is bein removed, and thus the foundations uv society is a bein broken up. I saw in Richmond fair wimmin who hed, in olden times, never known wat labor wuz, a washin dishes, and cookin their own vittles; and I saw men, who hed wunst lived luxuriously on the labor uv a hundred niggers, now drivin drays, and sellin dry goods and groceries, and sich, and my soul sunk within me. Wuz the cuss a mistake? Wuz the nigger not the race that wuz cussed? or has he becum so bleached, so lost in the white by amalgamation, that there ain't enough uv the black left in each indivijjle for the cuss to hang to.

Andrew Johnson! in your hands rests our cause; on your ackshen depends our weal or woe! Yoo, and yoo alone, kin remedy this. Wat if a corrupt and radikle Congress does override your vetoes, and legislate for these cuss-ridden people? Yoo hev yet a power wich yoo must not hesitate to make em feel. Clear out the rump Congress; declare our Southern brethren entitled to their seats, and see that they hev em. The Dimocrisy uv the North, wich wuz latterly for peece, are now fur war. They will sustain yoo. Reverse yoor ackshen, and yoo kin attach em to yoo with hooks uv steel. There ain't no risk in it — nary risk. Turn the Ablishnists out uv the Post Offices, and replace em with Democrats; let it be understood that yoo hev come back to your fust love, and no longer abide in the tents uv Ablishunism, — and all will be well. Talk less uv yoor policy, and put more uv it into acts. Combine Post Offices with Policy, and proclaim that only he who sustains the latter shel hev the former, and yoo kin depend on the entire Democrisy North. We are waitin anxiously. From the South comes up the cry, wich the North reëkkoes.

Will Androo Johnson, wich Ablishnists call Moses, but wich we, for obvious reasons, style the 2d Jaxon, heed that cry? or will he persist in clingin to the black idol he embraced four years ago?

PETROLEUM V. NASBY,

Lait Paster uv the Church uv the Noo Dispensashun.

XXI.

A Psalm of Gladness. — The Veto of the Civil Rights Bill, and other Matters, occasioning a Feeling of Thankfulness in the Minds of the Democracy.

CONFEDRIT X ROADS
(wich is in the Stait uv Kentucky),
May 1, 1866.

I AM a canary, a nightengale. A lark, am I.
I raise my voice in song. I pour forth melojus notes.

I am a lamb, wich frisketh, and waggeth his tale, and leapeth, ez he nippeth the tender grass. I am a colt, wich kicketh up its heels exuberantly.

I am a bridegroom, wich cometh from his bride in the mornin feelin releeved in the knowledge that she wore not palpitators, nor false calves, nor nothin false, afore she wuz hizn.

I am a steamboat captin with a full load, a doggry keeper on a Saturday nite, a sportin man with four aces in his hand.

All these am I, and more.

For we sought to establish ourselves upon a rock, but found that the underpinnin wuz gone out uv it.

Even slavery wuz our strong place, and our hope; but the corners hed bin knocked out uv it.

The sons uv Belial hed gone forth agin it. Massachusetts hed assailed it, and the North West hed drawd its bow agin it.

Wendell Phillips hed pecked out wun stun, Garret Smith another; and the soljers hed completed what they hed begun.

And Congris, even the Rump, hed decreed its death, and hed held forth its hand to Ethiopia.

It passed a bill givin the Niggers their rites, and takin away from us our rites:

Sayin, that no more shel we sell em in the market place,

Or take their wives from em,

Or be father to their children,

Or make uv em conkebines aginst their will,

Or force em to toil without hire,

Or shoot em, ez we wuz wont to do under the old dispensashun,

Or make laws for em wich didn't bind us as well.

And our hearts wuz sad in our buzzums; for we said, Lo! the nigger is our ekal; and we mourned ez them hevin no hope.

But the President, even Androo, the choice uv Booth, said, Nay.

And the bill wuz vetoed, and is no law ; and our hearts is made glad.

And from the Ohio to the Gulf shel go up the song uv gladness and the sounds uv mirth.

The nigger will we slay, for he elevated his horn agin us.

We will make one law for him and another for us, and he will sigh for the good old times when he wuz a slave in earnest.

His wife shel be our conkebine, ef she is fair to look upon ; and ef he murmurs, we'll bust his head.

His daughters shel our sons possess ; and their inkrease will we sell, and live upon the price they bring.

In our fields they shel labor ; but the price uv their toil shel make us fat.

Sing, O my soul !

The nigger hed become sassy and impudent, and denied that he wuz a servant unto his brethren.

He sheltered hisself behind the Freedman's Burow, and the Civil Rites Bill, and the soldiery, and he wagged his lip at us, and made mouths at us.

And we longed to git at him, but because of these we durst not.

But now who shell succor him.

We will smite him hip and thigh, onless he consents to be normal.

Our time uv rejoicin is come.

In Kentucky, the soldiers voted, — them ez wuz clothed in gray, — and we routed the Abolishnists.

Three great capchers hev we made : New Orleens we capcherd, Kentucky we capcherd, and the President — him who aforetime strayed from us — we capcherd.

Rejoice, O my soul! for yoor good time, wich wuz so long a comin, is come.

We shel hev Post Offisis, and Collectorships, and Assessorships, and Furrin Mishns, and Route Agencies, and sich ; and on the proceeds thereof will we eat, drink, and be merry.

The great rivers shel be whisky, the islands therein sugar, the streems tributary lemon joose and bitters, and the faithful shel drink.

Whisky shel be cheap ; for we shel hold the offises, and kin pay ; and the heart uv the barkeeper shel be glad.

The Ablishnist shel hang his hed ; and we will jeer him, and flout him, and say unto him, " Go up, bald head!" and no bears shel bite us; for, lo! the President is our rock, and in him we abide.

Blessed be Booth, who give us Androo.

Blessed be the veto, wich makes the deed uv Booth uv sum account to us.

Blessed be Moses, who is a leadin us out uv the wilderness, into the Canaan flowin with milk and honey.

PETROLEUM V. NASBY,
Lait Paster uv the Church of the New Dispensashun.

XXII.

The Reconstructed meet to Congratulate the Coun-
try upon the Result of the Memphis Outbreak.
— The Reverend discourses upon the Nigger,
and runs against a Snag.

CONFEDRIT X ROADS
(wich is in the Stait uv Kentucky),
May 12, 1866.

THE news from Memphis filled the soles uv the
Dimocrisy uv Kentucky with undilooted joy·
There, at last, the Ethiopian wuz taught that to
him, at least, the spellin book is a seeled volume,
and that the gospel is not for him, save ez he gits it
filtered through a sound, constooshnel, Dimekratic
preacher. We met at the Corners last nite to jollify
over the brave acts uv our Memphis frends, and I
wuz the speaker. I addressed them on the subjick
uv the nigger, — his wants, needs, and capacities, —
a subjick, permit me to state, I flatter myself I understand.

Probably no man in the Yoonited States hez

given the nigger more study, or devoted more time
to a pashent investigashen uv this species uv the
brute creashen, than the undersigned. I have contemplated him sittin and standin, sleepin and wakin,
at labor and in idleness, — in every shape, in fact,
ceptin ez a free man, wich situashen is too disgustin
for a proud Caucashen to contemplate him; and
when he ariz before my mind's eye in that shape, I
alluz turned shuddrin away.

I hed proceeded in my discourse with a flowin
sale. It's easy demonstratin anythin yoor awjence
wants to beleeve, and wich their interest lies in.
For instants, I hev notist wicked men, who wuz
somewhat wedded to sin, genrally lean toward Uni-
versalism; men heavily developed in the back uv
the neck are easily convinst uv the grand trooths uv
free love; and them ez is too fond uv makin money
to rest on the seventh day, hev serious doubts ez to
whether the observance uv the Sabbath is bindin
onto em. I, not likin to work at all, am a firm
beleever in slavery, and wood be firmer ef I cood
get start enuff to own a nigger.

I hed gone on and proved concloosively, from a
comparison uv the fizzikle structer uv the Afrikin
and the Caucashen, that the nigger wuz a beast, and
not a human bein; and that, consekently, we hed a

perfeck rite to catch him, and tame him, and yoose
him ez we do other wild animals. Finishin this
hed uv my discourse, I glode easily into a history
uv the flood ; explained how Noer got tite and cust
Ham, condemnin him and his posterity to serve his
brethren forever, wich I insisted give us an indubi-
table warranty deed to all uv em for all time.

I warmed up on this elokently. " Behold, my
brethren, the beginnin uv Dimocrasy," I sed. "Fust,
the wine (which wuz the antetype of our whisky)
wuz the beginnin. Wine (or whisky) wuz necessary to the foundation uv the party, and it wuz
forthcomin. But the thing was not complete. It
did its work on Noer, but yet there wuz a achin
void. There was no *Nigger* in the world, and
without nigger there could be no Dimocracy.
Ham, my friends, wuz born a brother uv Japhet,
and wuz like unto him, and, uv course, could not
be a slave. Whisky wuz the instrument to bring
him down ; and it fetched him. Ham looked upon
his father, and was cust ; and the void wuz filled.
There wuz Nigger and whisky, and upon
them the foundashuns uv the party wuz laid, broad
and deep. Methinks, my brethren, when Ham
went out from the presence uv his father, black in
the face ez the ace uv spades (ef I may be allowed

10

to yoose the expression), bowin his back to the bur-
dens Shem and Japhet piled onto him with alacrity,
that Democracy, then in the womb uv the future,
kicked lively, and clapped its hands.   There wuz a
nigger to enslave, and whisky to bring men down
to the pint uv enslavin him.   There wuz whisky to
make men incapable uv labor ; whisky to accom-
pany horse racin, and poker playin, and sich ra-
tional amoosements, and a nigger cust especially
that he mite sweat to furnish the means.   Observe
the fitniss uv things.   Bless the Lord, my brethren,
for whisky and the nigger ; for, without em, there
could be no Dimocrisy, and yoor beloved speaker
mite hev owned a farm in Noo Jersey, and bin a
votin the whig ticket to-day."

At this pint, a venerable old freedman, who wuz
a sittin quietly in the meetin, ariz, and asked ef he
mite ask a question.   Thinkin what a splendid op-
portoonity there wood be uv demonstratin the sooperiority uv the Caucashen over the Afrikin race, I
answered " Yes," gladly.

" Well, Mas'r," sed the old imbecile, " is I a
beest ?"

" My venerable friend, there ain't nary doubt
uv it."

" Is my old woman a old beastesses, too ?"

"Indubitably," replied I.

"And my children — is they little beasts and beastesses?"

"Onquestionably."

"Den a yaller feller ain't but a half a beast, is he?"

"My friend," sed I, "that question is —— "

"Hold on," sed he; "wat I wanted to git at is dis: dere's a heap uv yaller fellers in dis section, whose fadders must hev bin white men; and, ez der mudders wuz all beastesses, I want to know whedder dar ain't no law in Kentucky agin —— "

"Put him out!" "Kill the black wretch!" shouted a majority uv them who hed bin the heaviest slave owners under the good old patriarkle system, and they went for the old reprobate. At this pint, a officer uv the Freedmen's Bureau, who we hedn't observed, riz, and, bustin with laughter, remarked that his venerable friend shood have a chance to be heerd. We respeck that Burow, partikelerly ez the officers generally hev a hundred or two bayonets within reech, and, chokin our wrath, permitted ourselves to be further insulted by the cussed nigger, who, grinnin from ear to ear, riz and perceeded.

" My white friends," sed he, " dar pears to be an objection to my reference to de subjeck uv dis mixin with beasts, so I won't press de matter. But I ask yoo, did Noer hev three sons?"

" He did," sed I.

" Berry good.   Wuz dey all brudders?"

" Uv course."

" Ham come from the same fadder and mudder as the odder two?"

" C-e-r-t-i-n-l-y."

" Well, den, it seems to me — not fully understandin the skripters — dat if we is beasts and beastesses, dat you is beasts and beastesses also, and dat, after all, we is brudders."   And the disgustin old wretch threw his arms around my neck, and kissed me, callin me his " long lost brudder."

The officer uv the Freedmen's Bureau laft vosiferously, and so did a dozen or two soljers in the crowd likewise ; and the awjence slunk out without adjournin the meetin, one uv em remarkin, audibly, that he had noticed one thing, that Dimocrisy wuz extremely weak whenever it undertook to defend itself with fax or revelashun.   For his part, he'd done with argyment.   He wanted niggers, because he cood wallop em, and make em do his work without payin em, wich he coodent do with white men.

I left the meetin house convinst that the South, who worked the niggers, leavin us Northern Dimokrats to defend the system, hed the best end uv the bargain.

Petroleum V. Nasby,

Lait Paster uv the Church of the Noo Dispensashun.

XXIII.

The Workings of the Freedmen's Bureau.— A Report.

CONFEDRIT ✕ ROADS
(wich is in the Stait uv Kentucky),
May 27, 1866.

To His EGGSLENCY THE DISPENSER UV POST ORIFICES, ANDROO
JOHNSON, PRESIDENT UV THE UNITED STATES :

IN akordance with yoor esteemed request, dated
the 25th, and received this morning, I to-wunst
proceeded to make doo enquiry ez to the workin uv
the Freedmen's Burow, and the condishun uv the
Afrikin citizens uv Amerikin descent in this vicinity. The fact that a Ablishnist still holds the Post
Orifice at the Corners (wich place, by the way, I
hev been solicited to accept), interfered materially
with the bizines I hed in hand. I to-wunst tooted
the horn, ez is the custom when we hev religious
servis, and called my congregashun together. They
kum runnin in from the different groceries; and
here another difficulty ensood. The grosery keepers wanted to know what we wuz a going to hev

meetin on week days for? They wuz willin to
shut up doorin meetin time on Sundays, ez they
respected the church, and it give em time to sweep
out the terbacker, et settery; but they'd be d—d ef
they wuz a goin to hev the people pulled away from
their nourishment on week days. I succeeded in
pacifyin em, and went in at wunst examinin the
leadin citizens. Their testimony is ez follows: —

CAPTIN SKELPER

Wuz a nigger owner afore the war, and durin the
late fratrisidle struggle wuz a captan in the confedrit
servis. Wuz with Ginral Forest at Fort Pillow.
Hez hed much experence with niggers. Bleeves
em to be adapted to the climit uv Kentucky, and
much more able to stand the hot sun than the
whites. When they wuz slaves, never knowd em
to refooze to work; know they alluz did work,
becoz he generally stood over em with a nigger
whip. Since they hev bin free, hez notist a change;
not much uv a change, ontil the Nigger Burow wuz
establisht. Before that they'd take sich wages ez
yoo chose to give em; since then the d—d heathen
will stand out bout ez the white men do, and won't
work at all onless yoo meet their views, wich made
a heap up trouble, and materially retarded the devel-

ment uv the country. The Burow hed corrupted the female niggers ; ez they hed all bin legally married by the Chaplins to the men they'd lived with, and wuz so sot on livin with em, that there's no yoose uv yoor tryin to get a house wench unless yoo took her husband also. His wife wuz now doin degradin work at home for want uv help. Strongly urged the abrogashen uv the Burow, and the removal uv the Abolishun Postmaster at the Corners.

DEACON McGRATH

Wuz eggsamined. Wuz convinst in his own mind that the Afrikin wuz now out uv his normal speer, and that the infernal Burow wuz at the bottom uv it. The nigger, afore the Burow come around, wuz docile and easly controlled. His boy Joe wuz wunst a model nigger. He'd get up every mornin at 4 A. M. (wich means in the mornin), and work every day till after dark. Ez soon ez he wuz emancipated, ez they called it, and the Burow come, I told him to get up, one mornin ; and he told me, impudently, that he'd concluded he woodent. I undertook to chastise him with a fence stake, whereupon he sailed in, and whaled me ; and the Burow, to which I applied for redress, larft in my face. He left, and is now draggin out a mizerable existence in Ohio, on the beggarly pittance uv two dollars a day, and my farm is runnin to weeds. He conclooded by givin it ez his solemn opinion that he never cood be reconciled to the Government so long ez the Burow wuz tolerated, and that Ablishnist held the Post Orifis at the Corners.

Gineral Dinges

Considered the Burow a inkubus upon the State. It interfered between master and servant. Cood git along better ef the nigger wuz left to the nateral laws wich regulates capital and labor. Tried to keep his niggers, and did keep em the past summer till after the crop wuz in, and then tried to settle with em for four dollars a month, with sich deductions for food, sickness, and brakin tools, et settry, ez wuz just. Brought the niggers, all uv em, in my debt, and generously proposed to let em work it out choppin cord wood doorin the winter. Hauled me up afore the Burow, and wuz forst to pay em each $15 per month. Consider the Burow ez all that stands in the way uv rekonstruction, though the removal uv the Ablishun Postmaster at the Corners and the appintment uv a sound constooshnel Dimekrat wood grately assist in conciliatin the Kentucky mind.

I tried to get some nigger testimony, but cood elicit nothing worth while. One nigger, who spends the heft uv his time at the Corners, wuz opposed to the Burow becoz it stopt rations on him. And Lucy, a octoroon, who formerly belonged to, and still resides with, Elder Gavitt (who is now absent ez a delegate to a Southern religious convention at Louisville), testified that the Burow " wuz no grate shakes," becoz bein ez the Elder wuz a widower, and the father uv all her children, and bein she's a free woman, she askt the agent to make the Elder marry her, and he woodn't do it. But sich evidence is irrelevant, and I didn't consider it worth while botherin yoor Eggslency with it.   Both, however, strongly insisted on the removal uv the Ablishun Postmaster at the Corners.

ABSLUM PETTUS

Wuz convinst the Burow wuz agin the prosperity uv the State, and wuz underminin the moral and physikle welfare uv the nigger.   It made him impudent. Hed sum uv em workin for him, and notist at noons and nites he'd find em with a spellin-book and a reader. Didn't bleeve in readin. Coodent read hisself, but hed a cousin wunst who learned;

but ez soon ez he cood read he moved off to Inje-anny, quit the Democrisy, and becum a loathsum Ablishnist. Heerd he wuz killed in the war, and served him rite. Wanted to know what we wood do when the niggers cood all read. Sposed we'd hev to 'lect em to offis, ez the people alluz selected sich, when they cood find em. Didn't bleeve in nigger equality, and wuz in favor uv a imediate change in the post orfice at the Corners.

Captin McSlather thought things hed cum to a sweet old pass, when a man coodn't lather a nigger without bein hauled up afore a Burow.

Kurnel Pelter thought ef yoor Eggsolency cood witness the corupshun that eggsisted in the Burow, yoo'd make short work uv it. Why, he whipped a nigger hand more than he ought, perhaps, and he died uv the injuries. It wuz a aggravatin case. The nigger wuz sassy, and it cost three hundred and sixteen dollars to pervide for his family. That in-famous Burow made me pay for their rashens all winter. He asked, indignantly, ef this wuz or wuz not a free kentry into wich such things wuz permit-ted. And the Ablishen Postmaster at the Corners approved the tyranikle action. He demanded his removal.

I conceive it to be onnecessary to submit further testimony. I know not what luck yoor other commissioners may hev met with in takin testimony on this subjick; but in this vicinity there can't be no doubt that there can't be that love for the Government, without wich free instooshens won't flourish to any alarmin extent, ontil this monster is squelched. The testimony is unanimous, and them ez I hev eggsamined are representative men.

You may hev notist, also, the singler unanimity with wich they all bore testimony to the necessity uv a change in the Post Orifis at the Corners. I endorse all they say on this question, considerin that that change is ez necessary in the grate work uv pacifyin and consiliation ez is the removal of the Burow. In case a change is made, I would say, for your guidance, that I hev been warmly solicited by my friends to accept the position, and to pacify em, hev at last yielded a reluctant consent. The fact that I never served in the Confederate army may be an objection; but, to offset that, I voted for Vallandygum twice.

Ef possible, send me a pardon at the same time yoo send me my commission ez Post Master; for, if the Post Offis don't pay, I may want to run for some other office, in wich event that document would be essential to my success.

With sentiments uv the most profound respek,

I am

Trooly yours,

PETROLEUM V. NASBY,

Lait Paster uv the Church uv the Noo Dispensashun.

XXIV.

Presides at a Church Trial.

CONFEDRIT X ROADS
(wich is in the Stait uv Kentucky),
June 9, 1866.

THEY hed a ruction in the church at the Corners yisterday, wich bid fair to result in a rendin uv the walls of our Zion, and the tearin down uv the temple we hev reared with so much care and hev guarded with so much solissitood. When I say "we," I mean the members thereof, ez the church wuz reorganized sence the war by returned Confedrit soljers and sich Dimokrats ez remaned at home nootrel; but inasmuch ez I am the only reglerly ordained Dimokratic paster in these parts I ginerly conduct the services, and hentz hev insensibly fell into a habit uv speekin uv the church ez "my" church, and I feel all the solissitood for its spiritooal and temporal welfare that I cood ef I wuz reglerly ordained ez its paster, wich I expect to be ef I fail in gettin that post offis at the Corners,

wich is now held by a Ablishnist uv the darkest
dye, wich President Johnson, with a stubbornness I
can't account for, persistently refooses to remove.

The case wuz suthin like this : —

Deekin Pogram wuz charged by Elder Slather
with hevin, in broad daylite, with no attempt at
concealment, drunk with a nigger, and a free nigger
at that, in Bascom's grocery, and to prove the charge
Deekin Slather called Deekin Pennibacker.

The Deekin wuz put onto the stand, and testified
ez follows : —

" Wuz in Bascom's grocery a playin seven up for
the drinks with Deekin Slather.   Hed jist beet the
Deekin one game and hed four on the second, and
held high, low, and jack, and wuz modritly certin uv
goin out, partiklerly ez the Deekin didn't beg.   Wuz
hevin a little discussion with him — the Deekin insistin that it wuz the best three in five, instead uv
the best two in three, jest ez though a man cood
afford to play five games between drinks !   The ijee
is preposterous and unheard of, and ther ain't no
precedent for any sich course.   We wuz settlin the
dispoot in regler orthodox style — he hed his fingers
twisted in my neck handkercher, and I held a stick
uv stove wood suspended over his head.   While in
this position we wuz transfixed with horror at seein

Deekin Pogram enter, arm-in-arm with a nigger, and, —

The Court. — Arm-in-arm, did you say, Brother Pennibacker?

Witness. — Certainly.

The Court. — The scribe will make a minnit uv this. Go on.

Witness. — They cum in together, ez I sed, arm-in-arm, walked up to the bar, and drank together.

By the Court. — Did they drink together?

Witness. — They ondeniably did.

By myself. — The Court desires to know what partikeler flooid they absorbed.

Witness. — Can't say — spose 'twas Bascom's new whiskey — that's all he's got, ez the Court very well knows.

By myself. — The Sexton will go at once to Bascom's and procoor the identicle bottle from wich this wretched man, who stands charged with thus lowerin hisself, drunk, and bring it hither. The Court desires to know for herself whether it was really whisky. The pint is an important one for the Court to know.

A wicked boy remarked that the pint wood be better onderstood by the Court if it wuz a quart. The bottle wuz, however, brought, and the Court, wich is me, wuz satisfied that it wuz really and trooly whisky.   Ez the refreshin flooid irrigated my parched throat, I wished that trials based upon that bottle cood be perpetooal.

I considered the case proved, and asked Brother Pogram what palliation he hed to offer.   I set before him the enormity uv the crime, and showed him that he was by this course sappin the very foundashun uv the Church and the Democratic party. Wat's the use, I askt, uv my preachin agin nigger equality, so long ez my Deekins practis it?   I told him that Ham wuz cust by Noer, and wuz condemned to be a servant unto his brethren — that he wuz an inferior race, that the Dimocrisy wuz built upon that idea, and that associatin with him in any shape that indicated equality, wuz either puttin them up to our standard or lowrin ourselves to theirn ; in either case the result wuz fatal.   I implored Brother Pogram to make a clean breast uv it, confess his sin, and humbly receeve sich punishment ez shood be awarded him, and go and sin no more.   " Speak up, Brother Pogram," sez I, paternally, and yet severely.

Brother Pogram, to my unspeekable relief, for he is the wealthiest member of the congregashun, and one we darsn't expel, replied, —

"That he DID drink with the nigger, and wat wuz more, he wuz justified in doin it, for THE NIGGER PAID FOR THE WHISKY!!"

"But shoorly," I remarked, "it wasn't nessary to yoor purpose to come in with the nigger arm-in-arm, — a attitood wich implies familiarity, ef not affeckshun."

The Prisoner. — The nigger and I hed bin pitchin coppers for drinks, and I, possessin more akootnis, hed won. I took the nigger by the arm, fearin that ef I let go uv him he'd dodge without payin. They are slippery.

Overjoyed, I clasped him around the neck, and to-wunst dismist the charge as unfounded and frivo-lous.

"My brethren," sez I, "the action of Brother Pogram is not only justifiable, but is commendable, and worthy of imitashun. Ham wuz cust by Noer, and condemned by him to serve his brethren. The nigger is the descendant of Ham, and we are the descendants uv the brethren, and ef Noer hed a clear rite to cuss one of his sons, and sell him out to the balance uv the boys for all time, we hev ded wood on the nigger, for it is clear that he wuz made to labor for us and minister to our wants. So it wuz, my brethren, until an Ape, who hed power, inter-

fered and delivered him out of our hand.   Wat shel
we do?   Wat we cannot do by force we must do by
financeerin.   We can't any longer *compel* the nigger
to furnish us the means, and therefore in order to
fulfil the skripter, we are justified in accomplishing
by our sooperior skill wat we used to do with whips
and dorgs.

"The spectacle uv Brother Pogram's marchin
into Bascom's with that nigger wuz a sublime spectacle, and one well calculated to cheer the heart uv
the troo Dimekrat.   He hed vanquished him in an
encounter where skill wuz required, thus demonstratin the sooperiority uv the Anglo-Saxon mind —
he led him a captive, and made uv him a spoil.

"Wood, O wood that we all hed a nigger to play
with for drinks!   The case is dismissed, the costs to
be paid by the complainant!"

The walls uv our Zion is stronger than ever.
This trial, ez it resulted, is a new and strong abut-
ment — a tall and strong tower.

PETROLEUM V. NASBY,

Lait Paster uv the Church uv the Noo Dispensashun.

XXV.

Turns a Meeting, called to Indorse General Rosseau, to Account.

CONFEDRIT × ROADS
(wich is in the Stait uv Kentucky),
June 22, 1866.

THERE wuz joy at the Corners when the Post-master (who takes the only paper wich comes to the office, ceptin a few wich comes to some demoralized niggers who hev learned to read, and the officers uv the Freedmen's Burow here) read to the crowd the news uv the canin wich Rosso, wich is uv Kentucky, give Grinnell. It sent a thrill uv joy through the State, wich ain't done thrillin yet. Bustin out into nine harty cheers, we to-wunst organized a meetin for the purpose uv expressin our feelins on the momentous occasion. The bell wuz rung, the people gathered together, and I wuz elected Chairman (they alluz elect me to preside becoz I'm bald-hedded; they think bald heads and dignity is inseparable), and Deekin Pogram Secretary, with 36 Vice-Presidents — one for each State. I made a short speech on takin the chair, congratulatin em on the auspicious event wich called us together. Whereupon a Committee on Resolutions wuz appinted, wich, after a short absense, reported ez follows : —

Whereas, Genral Rosso, a native-born Kentuckian, and therefore a gentleman, hevin got into a argument with a Iowa sheep-breeder ; and,

Whereas, hevin got the wust uv the argument, he dextrously turned it into blackguardin ; and,

Whereas, hevin got the wust uv the blackguardin, he remembered the ancient usages uv the chivalrous sons uv the South, and caned him ; therefore, be it

Resolved, That we, the Dimocrisy uv Confedrit × Roads, wich is in the State uv Kentucky, hereby thank General Rosso for his manly vindication uv the character uv Kentucky.

Resolved, That we know not wich to admire the most ; the dashin Gineral's courage in bravin the public sentiment uv the North, or his prudence in selectin the smallest and physically weakest man in the House to demonstrate onto.

Resolved, That ez Thad Stevens is 70 years uv age, and lame, and hardly recovered from his fit uv sickness, we suggest that our beloved hero commence a argument with him, feelin that so far ez the argument and blackguardin goes the result will be the same, only so much more so ez to give him a good excuse for killin him, wich wood be doin the South a servis indeed.

Resolved, That the Dimocrisy uv Kentucky hevent felt so good sence the Memphis riots.

Resolved, That this manly act uv Gineral Rosso's makes up and compensates the South for the outrage he inflicted onto her when he jined the vandal host wich devastated her soil, and that hereafter he shel be receeved with just the same cordiality ez tho he had gone into the Confedrit instid uv the Federal servis.

Resolved, That the thanks uv the Dimocrisy are due the bold, brave men who accompanied and stood by General Rosso in this vindication uv the Southern spirit.

I put the affirmative, ez is the custom here, it bein the rool, when the leaders want a thing to pass, never to call for the nays, and it went through all right. Then I arose, and stated I hed another resolution, wich I wished to offer, and I read it : —

Resolved, That in retainin in the Post Offis, at the Corners, a Ablishnist, President Johnson is — "

At this point Deekin Pogram interrupted me. He spozed this meetin wuz called to congratulate Ginral Rosso, and wat wuz the sense uv mixin up a paltry Post Offis with a matter uv so much importance ez the canin uv a Ablishnist? It was clearly out uv order.

I replied, —

" Wood *yoo* be glad, or wood this congregashun be glad, to hev me in the Post Orfis in the place uv that Ablishnist? "

The Deekin replied that personally he wood. He had the highest respect for my massive talents and my excellent qualities uv head and heart, and besides, he thought probable, ef I got the Post Orfis, he wood stand a chance uv gettin the nine dollars and sixty-two cents borrowed money I owed him, and —

I called him to order at once.

Bascom, who keeps the grocery, and who furnishes me with likker (wich I hev to take for my hair) on the strength uv remittances I am to receeve, insisted on hearin the resolution ef it wood further my gettin the Post Orfis, and so did the benevolent gentleman with whom I board, and I resoomed, —

" I kin see a good reason for incorporatin a reso-
looshun demandin a change in the Post Orfis into
the proceedins uv this meetin. There wood be, my
friends," sed I, " no yoose uv sendin him a naked
resolution demandin this change, becoz he reseeves
hundreds and tens uv hundreds uv applications for
offices every day ; in fact, they pile in at sich a rate
that he never opens the half uv them. The Dimocrisy, my brethren, are alive on this subject. Ef
they are to support the President, they want, and
will hev, the post orifises, for uv what use is it to
support a man and pay yoor own expenses? It is
plain that the proceedins uv a post offis meetin
wood never reach him, but this, my brethren, goes
up to him from the PEOPLE, endorsin a supporter uv
his policy, and ez it will be the only one he hez
reseeved, or will reseeve, he will read it and read it
through, and in the exultation he will feel at bein
endorsed by anybody, who doubts the result? The
Post Orifis is mine."

Bascom, the grocery keeper, moved, excitedly,
the adoption uv the resolution. I suggested that I
hed better read it, but he sed it made no difference ;
he knew it wuz all rite. The benevolent and confidin individooal I board with seconded the motion,
and Deekin Pogram supported it in a short speech,

statin that he understood that it wuz Brother Nasby's intention, ef he succeeded in procoorin the position, to devote the first three and a half years' salary towards payin off the small indebtedness he hed contracted sence he hed honored the town by residin in it. To all uv wich I blandly smiled an assent, whereupon the resolution wuz adopted yoonanimusly. Hevin lived here a little risin uv a year, the vote wuz perfeckly yoonanimous.

My prospex is britenin.

PETROLEUM V. NASBY,

Lait Paster uv the Church uv the Noo Dispensashun.

XXVI.

Preaches — The "Prodigal Son" — An Interruption.

CONFEDRIT X ROADS
(wich is in the Stait uv Kentucky),
July 6, 1866.

I PREACHED last Sabbath, or rather, tried to, from the parable of the Prodigal Son. We hed a splendid congregashun. I notice a revival of the work in this part uv the Dimocratic vineyard wich reely cheers me. The demonstrashun our friends made in Memphis, the canin uv Grinnel by Rosso, and the call for a Johnson Convenshun in Philadelphia, all, all hev conspired to comfort the souls uv the Dimocrisy, and encourage em to renewed effort. It is bringing forth fruit. Only last week five northern men were sent whirlin out of this section. They dusted in the night to escape hangin, leavin their goods as a prey for the righteous. Six niggers hev bin killed and one Burow officer shot. Trooly there is everything to encourage us.

The house wuz full. The weather wuz hot, and

the pleasant incense uv mingled whiskey, tobacco, and snuff wich ariz wuz grateful to me. The sun shone in on Deekin Pogram's face ez he gently slept, and when the sun hits him square I kin alluz tell wher he sets, even ef it is dark. He drinks apple-jack instead of corn whiskey, and chaws fine cut tobacker instead uv plug, and consekently when in the pulpit I kin distinguish the pecooliar aroma uv his breath from those around him.

" My brethren," sed I, " sich uv yoo ez hev Bibles in yoor houses, kin get somebody to read yoo the parable to wich I shel call yoor attention. A man, wunst upon a time, hed sons, ez many men hev since, and wun uv em wuz a tough one. He left his home and went into far countries, makin the old man shel out his share uv the estate, and he lived high, jist, my brethren, ez yoor boys do, or rather, did, when they went to Noo Orleans, in the days when yoo hed a nigger or two wich yoo cood sell to supply em with money. He played draw poker and faro ; he drank fancy drinks, and boarded at big hotels ; and he follered after strange women, wich 'll bust a man quicker nor any one small sin the devil hez yet invented, ez yoor pastor kin testify. Uv course, his pile give out, and he got down, my friends, did this ingenuous yooth, to rags and wretchedness, and ended in being an overseer uv swine. What did he do? He ariz and went to his father, and the old man saw him afar off, and went out to meet him, and fell onto his neck, and give him a order for a soot of clothes and a pair uv boots, and put a ring onto his finger, and made a feast, killin for the purpose the fatted calf wich he hed saved for another occasion.

" My friends, you kin find in the Skripter suthin applicable to every occasion, and this parable fits the present time like a ready-made coat. The South is the Prodigal Son. We went out from our father's house on a expedition wich heznt proved altogether a success. We spent our share uv the estate, and a little more. We run through with our means, and hev cum down to rags, and dirt, and filth, and hunger. We are, and hev bin some time, a chawin husks. We run out after them twin harlots, Slavery and State Rights, and they've cleaned us out. Our pockets are empty. No more doth the pleasant half-dollar jingle in sweet unison agin its fellows. Our wallets is barren uv postal currency, and the grocery-keepers mourn, and refuse to be comforted, becoz we are not. We hev got to the husk stage uv our woe, and wood be tendin hogs, ef the armies, wich past through these countries, hed left us any.

We hev kum back. In rags and dirt we hev wended our way to Washington, and ask to be taken back. Now, why don't our father, the Government, fulfil the Skripter? Why don't it see us afar off, and run out to meet us? Why don't it put onto us a purple robe? Where's the ring for our finger, and the shoes for our feet? and where's the fatted calf he ought to kill? My brethren, them Ablishnists is worse than infiddles — while they preach the gospel they won't practise it. For my part, I —— "

At this point a sargent, belongin to that infernal Burow, who wuz in the awdience, with enough uv soldiers to make opposin uv him unpleasant, sed he hed bin a sort uv an exhorter in his day, and desired to say a word in explanation uv that parable, ez applicable to the present time ; and, sez he, " ef I am interrupted, remember I b'long to the church military, wich is, just now, the church triumphant." And cockin his musket he proceeded, very much uninterrupted.

" The prodigal son," sez he, " wuz received by the old man with considerable doins, but, my worthy friends, he went out decently. He didn't, ez soon ez he withdrawed from the house, turn around and make war onto the old gentleman — he didn't burn his house and barns, tear up his garden, burn his fences, and

knock down the balance uv the children.   Not any.
He went away peaceably, a *misguided* good-for-
nothin, but yet a *peaceable* good-for-nothin.   Secondly, he come back uv his own akkord.   The old
man didn't go after him, and fight for four years, at
a cost uv half his substance, to subdue him and
bring him back, but when he hed run through his
pile, and squandered his share uv the estate, and got
hungry, he came back like a whipped dog.

" My friends, let me draw a small parallel between
these cases.

" The Prodigal Son went out, — so did the South,
— thus farly the cases is alike.

" The Prodigal didn't steal nothin.   The Confederacy took everything it cood lay its hands on.

" The Prodigal spent only what wuz his to spend.
The Confederacy spent not only all it stole, but all
it cood borrer, when it knowd its promises to pay
wuzent worth the mizable paper they wuz printed
onto.

" The Prodigal, when he did come, come ez peni-
tent ez the consciousness that he hed made a fool
uv hisself cood make him.   The Confederacy wuz
whipped back, but it still swears hefty oaths that it
wuz right all the time.

" The Prodigal didn't *demand* veal pot-pies, and

purple robes, and sich, but begged to be a servant unto the more sensible brethren wich stayed. The South comes back *demandin* office, uv wich the fatted calf, and rings, and purple robes is typical, and considerably more share in the government than it had before it kicked over the traces, and went out like the lost tribes uv Israel.

" Spozn the Bible prodigal hed stopped his parient, and remarked to him thus : ' I am willin to come back, on conditions. Yoo must pay my debts — yoo must give me an ekal share uv the farm with the other boys — yoo must treat me in all respecks just ez ef I hadn't gone out, and — this is essential — yoo must take with me all the sharpers who ruined me, all the gamblers and thieves with whom I fell in while I wuz away, and make them head men on the place ; and above all, I hev with me the two harlots wich wuz the prime cause of my ruin, and they must hev eleven of the best rooms in the house, and must be treated ez your daughters. To avoid displeasin the others, I'll dress em in different clothes, but here they must stay. Otherwise, I'll go out agin.'

" Probably the old gentleman wood hev become indignant, and would hev remarked to him to go, and never let him see his audacious face agin, or rather, he would hev strangled the harlots, scattered the blacklegs, and choked the young sprout into submission. Them's me. I am anxious to kill that fatted calf, and am also anxious to put on yoo robes and shoes. But, alas! the calf suffered from want uv attention so long doorin the late misunderstandins that he's too poor — the robes wuz all cut up into bloo kotes for the soljers we sent out to fetch you in — the shoes they wore out, and the rings — Jeff'son Davis wears the only style we hev. When you come back in good shape, yool find us ready to meet you; but till then, chaw husks!"

Lookin around, this armed tyrant remarked that there would be no more preaching that day, and sadly the congregation dispersed.

I'm heart sick. At every turn I make that Burow stares me in the face, and counteracts my best endeavors. It's curious, though, what different sermons kin be preached from the same text, and it's also curious how quiet our folks listen to a ablishnist who hez muskets to back him.

PETROLEUM V. NASBY,
Lait Paster uv the Church of the New Dispensashun.

XXVII.

A Pleasant Dream, the Philadelphia Convention being the Subject thereof.

CONFEDRIT X ROADS
(wich is in the Stait uv Kentucky),
July 28, 1866.

MY dreams, uv wich I hev hed many doorin the past five years, hevent bin overly pleasant; indeed, they hev taken more the shape uv hideous nitemares than anything else — Linkin, Grant, Sherman, and armies dressed in blue, figurin extensively therein. But last nite I hed a vision wich more than repaid me for all I hev suffered heretofore. I hed bin at the Corners assistin in inauguratin a new grocery. The proprietor wuz a demoralized Ablishnist who hed sold likker surreptitiously in Maine, among them Ablishunists, and consekently hed no idea uv the quantity a full grown Kentucky Democrat cood throw hisself outside uv. His entire capital with which he proposed to commence biznis wuz one barrel uv new corn whiskey,

12

and some other necessaries, and ez a starter, to
make the acquaintance uv his customers, he announced one free nite, and invited the entire community.   His invitashun wuz considered generous,
and we met it in the same noble sperit — in a
more nobler sperit than the confidin and ignorant
man desired, in fact; for when we got through, in
about 38 minits, there wuzn't a drop uv the whiskey
left, and while the new grocery keeper wuz a rollin
uv us out, he wuz cussin hisself for a fool.   He
didn't open agin; he consoomed his stock in trade
in givin the blow-out to sekoor customers.   His
stock, like A. Johnson's Unionism, didn't survive an
inaugerashen.

I succumbed in a fence corner, and overpowered
ez I wuz, slept

> "A sweetly dreamin —
> Dreamin the happy hours away."

Methought I wuz in Philadelphia, and the 14th uv
August had arriv.   There wuz a glorious assemblage, ez Doolittle sed, uv the brains and hearts uv
the country, and I may add, ez I and Humphrey
Marshall wuz there, uv the bowels likewise.   The
Convenshun wuz assemblin.   There wuz Seward
present, engineerin uv it.   On one side uv him I

notist, in my dream, a shadowy bein with wings, draped in white, and wearin a melonkoly look, with one hand a layin on his shoulder, a tryin to take him out uv the hall, while another bein, with wings like a bat, hed him by the nose, and wuz a twistin uv him jest ez he desired. I notist that this last mentioned bein hed hoofs, wich wuz split, and a tail wich he wuz flirtin in great glee. The bein with the tail and hoofs whispered suthin in Seward's ear, whereupon he moved that that eminent patriot, Ex-President FRANKLIN PIERCE, be chairman; upon wich the shadowy bein in white unfolded her wings, and flew away, castin at William the most sorrowful look I ever saw, the hoofed and tailed individooal laughin tremendous. The Ex-President took the chair, and one Vice-President wuz appointed from each State, ceptin Vermont and Massachoosits. My buzzum swelled with emoshen ez that list wuz read; it wuz more like an old-fashioned Democratic Convenshun than anything I hed heard for five long years. I heard the honored names uv Toombs and Rhett, Pryor and Lee, Slidell and Rosso, and Dandridge and Forrest; I heard the names uv Craven and Pollard, Thompson and Forsyth, and I felt like him uv old — "Mine eyes hev seen thy glory, now let thy servant depart in peace." Nothin but the certainty that I wood at last hev that Post Offis at the Corners kept me from goin up. Singler 'tis wat slender ties hold us to earth !

The Secretaries wuz apinted, and then the committees — two on each from the South and one from the North, wich wuz consiliatin. I wuz put on the committee on credenshals, Randall, the Postmaster-General, bein the Northern representative. We hed our hands full. There wuz a rush made on us, so many claimin seats that we locked the doors for two hours to decide what shood be the proper qualification for a place. Finally we agreed to admit ez delegates, —

FROM THE NORTH — all Dimocrats who had bin arrested by Linkin's minyuns; all officers who hed resined rather than to serve in a Ablishun war, and all Republikins who cood show a commishun ez Postmaster and sich, and (this wuz considered necessary to guard agin imposition) who wuz willin to take his solemn oath that he wuz a steadfast bleever in everything A. Johnson hed did sence Janooary, '66 (ceptin sum small items wich wuz specified), and all he wuz doin, and all he mite do.

FROM THE SOUTH — all who cood show a officer's commission in the late Confedrit army ; all who had receeved a pardon from A. Johnson, and all

who hed lost their niggers in an unholy war, wich
inclooded all present.

This decided upon, the work wuz done. The
delegates took their seats, and the grate work uv
Reconstructin the Yoonyun commenced. Garret
Davis wanted to make a speech, and a hall wuz
hired for him in another part uv the city, and fifty
or sixty German emigrants, who coodent understand
a word uv English, hired at a shillin an hour to act
ez audience. Five kegs uv lager beer, a flooid wich
I hev bin told Germans tie to, hed bin rolled in the
hall, and most uv em stayed seven hours and a
half.

In the regler Hall there wuz a comminglin which
wuz edifyin. Doolittle wood make a motion, and
Vallandigham wood second it. Forrest made a
speech, and Randall indorsed it. Seward and John
Morrissey were on the Committee on Resolutions,
and Dick Taylor and Cowan were occupyin one
seat. The resolutions were brief and to the pint.
They resolved that, —

Whereas, there hed bin a season uv unpleasantness in our national history, wich, owin to circumstances over wich nobody hed any control, extended
over several periods uv ninety days each ; and

Whereas, the unpleasantness resulted from the two sections viewin things each from its own stand-pint, instead of viewin things from the other's stand-pint; and

Whereas, both parties wuz highly in the wrong, partikelerly the North; and

Whereas, the South, with a magnanimity unknown in history, hed thrown down her arms, and wuz ready to resoom her old position in the Government — nay, more, to take more than her old share in the trouble uv runnin the Government; therefore be it

Resolved, That we are for the Yoonyun ez it wuz.

Resolved, That the persistency uv a sectional Congress, in continuin the unpleasantness wich hez to some extent disturbed our system uv Government, in legistatin while eleven sovereign States is unrep-resented, is pizen.

Resolved, That we view with alarm the manifest determination uv Congress to centralize in their-selves the law-makin power uv the Government, and we pledge our support to our worthy Chief Magistrate, who is a second Jaxon, in his efforts to check their centralizin schemes by vetoin all they may do.

Resolved, That all traces uv the late onpleasant-ness may be wiped out ez soon ez possible, we demand uv Congress an appropriation for plowin over all the fields on wich the citizens uv the two sections who wuz indoost by their respective Governments, so-called, to carry muskets, cum together, particklerly them on wich our Southern brethren got the worst uv the disputes that ensood.

Resolved, That Congress shood, ez soon ez it convenes, change the names uv Murfreesboro', Gettysburg, Atlanta, Vicksburg, et settry, to sich names ez Smithboro', Brownsburg, Jonesburg, et settry, that the serious unpleasantnesses wich occurred at them places may be remembered no more forever.

Resolved, That the citizens uv the Southern States wich lost their lives, and legs, and sich, in the late unpleasantnesses wich hez bin referred to, ought to be placed on the pension rolls the same ez the Northern citizens who suffered likewise ; and that the debt incurred by the South in upholdin things ez viewed from its stand-pint, is entitled to be paid the same ez the debt incurred by the North in upholdin things ez viewed from its stand-pint.

Resolved, That we are willin, for the sake uv harmony, to admit that Sherman and Grant were, all things considered, worthy uv bein ranked with Lee and Jackson.

Resolved, That the safety uv the Government
demands that sich ez took part in the late unpleas-
antnis, from the Southern States, be to-wunst admitted to Congress, and to the other posishens wich
they yoost to ornament, and that the more unpleasant they wuz doorin the trouble the more they
ought to be admitted.

Resolved, That there shall be gushen confidences,
we freely forgive the honored Secretary uv State for
the too free use uv his little bell doorin the late un-
pleasantnis, believin that he viewed things from his
own stand-pint instead uv somebody else's, wich
alluz causes trouble.

At this pint His Eggslency, Andrew Johnson,
supported by Secretary Wells on the wun side and
Vice-President Stephens on one other, with Bukanan
in front and Toombs behind, entered the hall.   Sich
a cheering I never heerd.   Hats wuz slung into the
air, and seats wuz torn up.   Proudly they advanced
up the aisle, treading, ez they went, onto a portrait
uv Linkin wich a enthusiastic Connecticut delegate
tore from the wall and throwd before em.   They
took their position on the stage, Gen. Buell holdin
over em a Fedral flag, and Genral Henry A. Wise,

Nasby's Dream of the Philadelphia Convention. Page 185.

uv Virginny, a Confedrit flag, both wavin em to the music uv two bands; one a playin Dixie, and the other Yankee Doodle.

At this pint methought the sperit uv Washinton floated into the hall, and for a minnit contemplated the countenance uv President Johnson. In my dreem I heerd him murmur, " There wuz me, and Adams, and Gefferson, and Monroe, and sich, and then cum Fillmore, and Peerce, and Bookannon, and, good God! Johnson! Faugh!" and I notist that George spit ez tho' suthin in his mouth didn't taste well. In fact, the Father uv his country looked sick, and spreadin his wings, the sperit moved out uv the hall, shakin the sperit dust off uv his speritool boots ez he shot thro' the sky-lite.

There wuz then a blank in my dream. When I resoomed, I was at the Post-offis Department the next mornin. The gullotin hed commenced work, and the supporters uv the constitushun were reseevin their commissions ez postmasters ez fast ez four hundred clerks cood make em out. Ez I pressed forward, Randall hisself give me mine. " Take it, my venerable friend," sez he, with tears a gushin down his cheeks; " take it. No more shall that Demokrat in your township who takes a paper

reseeve it contaminated by the touch uv a Ablishin
radical."

At this critical pint I awoke. Wood that that
dream wuz a reality! Will I only git that postoffis
in a dream.

PETROLEUM V. NASBY,
Lait Paster uv the Church uv the Noo Dispensashun.

XXVIII.

*The Reward of Virtue. — After Months of wait-
ing, the Virtuous Patriot secures his Loaf. —
The Jollification.*

CONFEDRIT X ROADS
(wich is in the Stait uv Kentucky),
August 12, 1866.

A T last I hev it! Finally it come! After five
weary trips to Washington, after much weary
waitin and much travail, I hev got it. I am now
Post Master at Confedrit X Roads, and am dooly
installed in my new position. Ef I ever hed any
doubts ez to A. Johnson bein a better man than
Paul the Apossle, a look at my commission removes
it. If I ketch myself a feelin that he deserted us
onnecessarily five years ago, another look, and my
resentment softens into pity. Ef I doubt his Democrisy, I look at that blessed commission, and am
reassured, for a President who cood turn out a
wounded Federal soldier, and apoint sich a man ez
ME, must be above suspicion.

I felt it wuz coming two weeks ago. I received a

cirkler from Randall, now my sooperior in offis, propoundin these questions: —

1. Do yoo hev the most implicit faith in Androo Johnson, in all that he hez done, all that he is doin, and all he may hereafter do?

2. Do you bleeve that the Philadelphia Convenshun will be a convocashen uv saints, all actuated by pure motives, and devoted to the salvation uv our wunst happy, but now distractid country?

3. Do yoo bleeve that, next to A. Johnson, Seward, Doolittle, Cowan, and Randall are the four greatest, and purest, and bestest, and self-sacrificinest, and honestest, and righteousist men that this country hez ever prodoost?

4. Doo yoo bleeve that there is a partikelerly hot place reserved in the next world for Trumbull, a hotter for Wade, and the hottest for Sumner and Thad Stevens?

5. Do yoo approve uv the canin uv Grinnell by Rosso?

6. Do yoo consider the keepin out uv Congris eleven sovrin states a unconstooshnel and unwarrantid assumption uv power by a secshnal Congris?

7. Do yoo bleeve the present Congris a rump, and that (eleven states bein unrepresented) all their acts

are unconstooshnel and illegal, ceptin them wich provides for payin salaries?

8. Do yoo bleeve that the Memphis and Noo Orleans unpleasantnesses wuz brot about by the unholy machinashens uv them Radical agitators, actin in conjunction with ignorant and besotted nig-gers, to wreak their spite on the now loyal citizens uv those properly reconstructed cities.

9. Are yoo not satisfied that the African citizens uv Amerikin descent kin be safely trusted to the operations uv the universal law wich governs labor and capital?

10. Are yoo willin to contribute a reasonable per cent. uv yoor salary to a fund to be used for the defeat uv objectionable Congrismen in the disloyal states North?

To all uv these inquiries I not only answered yes, but went afore a Justis uv the Peace and took an affidavit to em, forwarded it back, and my commis-sion wuz forthwith sent to me.

There wuz a jubilee the nite it arriv. The news spread rapidly through the four groceries uv the town, and sich anuther spontaneous outbust uv joy I never witnessed.

The bells rung, and for an hour or two the

Corners wuz in the wildest stait uv eggsitement.
The citizens congratoolated each other on the certainty uv the acceshun uv the President to the
Dimocrisy, and in their enthoosiasm five nigger
families were cleaned out, two uv em, one a male
and the tother a female, wuz killed. Then a perceshun wuz organized as follers: —

Two grocery keepers with bottles.

Deekin Pogram.

ME, with my commishun pinned onto a banner,
and under it written, " In this Sign we Conker."

Wagon with tabloo onto it: A nigger on the
bottom boards, Bascom, the grocery keeper, with
one foot onto him, holdin a banner inscribed, " The
Nigger where he oughter be."

Citizen with bottle.

Deekin Pogram's daughter Mirandy in a attitood
uv wallopin a wench. Banner: " We've Regained
our Rites."

Two citizens with bottles tryin to keep in perceshun.

Two more citizens, wich hed emptyd their bottles,
fallin out by the way side.

Citizens, two and two, with bottles.

Wagon, loaded with the books and furnitur uv a
nigger skool, in a stait uv wreck, with a ded nigger

SUPPORTERS OF "MY POLICY" IN PROCESSION. Page 190.

layın on top uv it, wich hed bin captoored within
the hour. Banner: "My Policy."

The perceshun mooved to the meetin hous, and
Deekin Pogram takin the Chair, a meetin wuz to
wunst organized.

The Deekin remarked that this wuz the proudest
moment uv his life. He wuz gratified at the appintment uv his esteemed friend, becoz he appreciated the noble qualities wich wuz so conspikuous
into him, and becoz his arduous services in the coz
uv Dimokrisy entitled him to the posishun. All
these wuz aside uv and entirely disconnected from
the fact that thare wood now be a probability uv his
gittin back a little matter uv nine dollars and sixty-
two cents ("Hear! hear!") wich he hed loaned
him about eighteen months ago, afore he had
knowed him well, or larned to luv him. But thare
wuz anuther reason why he met to rejoyce to-nite.
It showed that A. Johnson meant bizness; that A.
Johnson wuz troo to the Dimokrasy, and that he
hed fully made up his mind to hurl the bolts uv
offishl thunder wich he held in his Presidenshal
hands at his enemies, and to make fight in earnest;
that he wuz goin to reward his friends — them ez
he cood trust. Our venerable friend's bein put in
condishun to pay the confidin residents uv the Cor-

ners the little sums he owes them is a good thing
(" Hear ! " " Hear ! " " Troo ! " " Troo ! " with
singular unanimity from every man in the bildin),
but wat wuz sich considerashuns when compared to
the grate moral effect uv the decisive movement?
("A d—d site ! " shouted one grocery keeper, and
" We don't want no moral effect ! " cried another.)
My friends, when the news uv this bold step uv the
President goes forth to the South, the price uv Confedrit skript will go up, and the shootin uv niggers
will cease ; for the redempshun uv the first I consider ashoored, and the redoosin uv the latter to
their normal condishun I count ez good ez done.

Squire Gavitt remarked that he wuz too much
overpowered with emoshun to speak. For four
years, nearly five, the only newspaper wich come
to that offis hed passed thro' the polluted hands uv
a Ablishnist. He hed no partikler objecshun to the
misguided man, but he wuz a symbol uv tyranny,
and so long ez he sot there, he reminded em that
they were wearin chains. Thank the Lord, that
day is over ! The Corners is redeemed, the second
Jaxson hez risin, and struck off the shackles. He
wood not allood to the trifle uv twelve dollars and
a half that he loaned the appintee some months
ago, knowin that it wood be paid out uv the first
money —

Bascom, the principal grocery keeper, rose, and called the Squire to order. He wanted to know ef it wuz fair play to talk sich talk. No man cood feel a more hart-felt satisfaction at the appintment uv our honored friend than him, showin, ez it did, that the President hed cut loose from Ablishnism, wich he dispised, but he protestid agin the Squire undertakin to git in his bill afore the rest hed a chance. Who furnisht him his licker for eight months, and who hez the best rite for the first dig at the proceeds uv the position? He wood never —

The other three grocery keepers rose, when Deekin Pogram rooled em all out uv order, and offered the followin resolutions : —

Whereas, the President hez, in a strikly constooshnel manner, relieved this commoonity uv an offensive Ablishunist, appinted by that abhorred tyrant Linkin, and appinted in his place a sound constooshnel Demokrat — one whom to know is to lend ; therefore, be it

Resolved, That we greet the President, and ashoor him uv our continyood support and confidence.

Resolved, That we now consider the work uv Reconstruction, so far ez this community is concerned, completed, and that we feel that we are wunst more restored to our proper relations with the federal government.

Resolved, That the glorious defence made by the loyal Democracy uv Noo Orleans agin the combined conventioners and niggers, shows that freemen kin not be conkered, and that white men shel rule America.

Resolved, That, on this happy occasion, we forgive the Government for what we did, and cherish nary resentment agin anybody.

The resolutions wuz adopted, and the meetin adjourned with three cheers for Johnson and his policy.

Then came a scene. Every last one uv em hed come there with a note made out for the amount I owed him at three months. Kindness of heart is a weakness of mine, and I signed em all, feelin that ef the mere fact of writin my name wood do em any good, it wood be crooel in me to object to the little laber required. Bless their innocent soles! they went away happy.

The next mornin I took possesshun uv the offis.

"Am I awake, or am I dreamin?" thought I. No, no! it is no dream. Here is the stamps, here is the blanks, and here is the commisshun!   It is troo! it is troo!

I heerd a child, across the way, singin, —

> "I'd like to be a angel,
> And with the angels stand."

I woodn't, thought I.   I woodn't trade places with an angel, even up.   A Offis with but little to do, with four grocerys within a stone's throw, is ez much happiness ez my bilers will stand without bustin.   A angel 4sooth!

PETROLEUM V. NASBY, P. M.

(wich is Postmaster.)

XXIX.

The Convocation of Hungry Souls at Philadel-
phia. — A Description of that Memorable Occa-
sion by One who had been Provided for.

POST OFFIS, CONFEDRIT X ROADS
(wich is in the Stait uv Kentucky),
August 14, 1866.

PEACE is into me. I hev spent many happy
periods in the course uv a eventful life; but I
never knowd what perfeck satisfaction wuz till now.
The first week I wuz married to my Looizer Jane it
wuz hevenly ; for, independent uv the other blisses
incident to the married state, I beleeved that she
wuz the undivided possessor uv a farm, or ruther her
father wuz, wich, on the old man's decease, wood be
hern, and the prospeck uv a lifetime with a amiable,
well-built woman, with a farm big enough to support me, with prudence on her part, wuz bliss itself;
and I enjoyed it with a degree uv muchness rarely
ekaled, until I found out that it wuz kivered more
deeply with mortgages than it wuz ever likely to be

with crops, and my dreem uv happiness busted. Sweet ez wuz this week, it wuz misery condensed when compared to the season I hev jest passed through.

I wuz a delegate to Philadelphia. I wuzn't elected nor nothin, and hedn't any credentials; but the door uv the wigwam I passed, nevertheless. The door-keeper wuz a Dimokrat, and my breath helped me; my nose, wich reely blossoms like the lobster, wuz uv yoose; but I spect my hevin a gray coat on, with a stand up collar, with a brass star onto it, wuz wat finished the biznis. The Southern delegates fought shy uv me; but the Northern ones, bless their souls! the minit they saw the star on the collar uv my gray coat, couldn't do enuff for me. They addressed me ez Kernel and Gineral, and sed " this wuz trooly an unmeritid honor," and paid for my drinks; and I succeeded in borrowin a hundred and twenty dollars of em the first day. I mite hev doubled it; but the fellows wuz took in so easy that no financeerin wuz required, and it really wuz no amoozment.

The Convenshun itself wuz the most affectinist gatherin I ever witnist. I hed a seat beside Randall, who wuz a managin the concern, and I cood see it all. The crowd rushed into the bildin, and

filled it, when Randall desired attention. He bein
the Postmaster General, every one of em dropped
into his seat ez though he hed bin shot, and there
wuz the most perfeck quiet I ever saw. Doolittle,
who wuz the Cheerman, winked at Randall, and
nodded his head, when Randall announced that THE
DELEGATES FROM SOUTH KARLINY, AND THE DEL-
EGATES FROM MASSACHOOSITS, WOOD ENTER ARM
IN ARM! With a slow and measured step they cum
in; and, at a signal from Randall, the cheerin commenst — and sich cheerin! Then Doolittle pulled
out his white hankercher, and applied it to his
eyes; and every delegate simultaneously pulled out
a white hankercher, and applied it to his eyes.

To me, this wuz the proudest moment uv my life;
not that there wuz anything partikilerly inspiritin in
the scene afore me, for there wuzzent. Orr, from
South Caroliny, looked partikilerly ashamed of hisself, ez though he wuz going thro a highly nessary,
but extremely disgustin, ceremony, and wuz determined to keep up a stiff upper lip over it; and
Couch looked up to Orr, ez though he wuz afeerd
uv him, and ez though he felt flattered by Orr's con-
decension in walkin at all with sich a umble indi-
vidjooal. But, to my eyes, the scene wuz signifi-
cant. I looked into the fucher, and wat did I see,

ez them two men — one sneekin, and tother ashamed uv hisself — walked up that aisle? Wat did I see? I saw the Democrisy restored to its normal condishun. I saw the reunion uv the two wings. In fact, I saw the entire Dimokratic bird reunited. The North, one wing, and the weakest; Kentucky, the beak, sharp, hungry, and rapacious; South-west, the strong, active wing; Virginny, the legs and claws; Ohio, the heart; Pennsylvania, the stomach; South Caroliny, the tail feathers; and Noo Jersey, the balance of the bird, — I saw these parts, for five years dissevered, come together, holdin nigger in one claw, and Post Offises in the other, sayin, "Take em both together; they go in lots." I saw the old Union — the bold, shivelrous Southner a guidin, controllin, and directin the machine, and assoomin to hisself the places uv honor, and the Dimokrat uv the North follerin, like a puppy dog, at his heels, takin sich fat things ez he cood snap up; the Southerner ashamed uv his associations, but forced to yoose em; the Northerner uncomfortable in his presence, but tied to him by self-interest. I saw a comin back the good old times when thirty-four States met in convenshun, and let eleven rule em; and ez I contemplated the scene, I too wept, but it wuz in dead earnest.

" Wat are you blubberin for? " asked a enthusiastic delegate in front uv me, who wuz a swabbin his
eyes with a handkercher.

" I'm a Postmaster," sez I, " and must do my
dooty in this crisis. Wat are you sheddin pearls
for? " retorted I. " Are you a Postmaster? "

" No," sez he ; " but I hope to be ; " and he
swabbed away with renood vigger.

" Wat's the matter with the eyes uv all the delegates? " sez I.

" They've all got Post Offisis in em," sez he ; and
he worked away faster than ever.

While gettin a fresh handkercher (wich I borrered
from the hind coat pocket uv a delegate near me,
and wich, by the way, in my delirious joy, I forgot
to say anythin to him about it), I looked over the
Convenshun, and agin the teers welled up from my
heart. My sole wuz full and overflowin, and I
slopped over at the eyes. There, before me, sat
that hero, Dick Taylor, and Cuth Bullitt ; and there
wuz the Nelsons and Yeadons, and the representatives uv the first families uv the South, and in PHIL-
ADELPHIA, AT A CONVENTION, with all the leadin
Demokrats uv the North, ceptin Vallandigham and
Wood, and they wuz skulkin around within call,
with their watchful eyes on the perceedins. Here

is a prospeck! Here is fatnis! The President into
our confidence! The Postmaster General a runnin
the Convention! The bands a playin Dixie and the
Star Spangled Banner alternitly, so that nobody
cood complain uv partiality, or tell reely wich side
the Convention wuz on, or wich side it had been on
in the past! Ah! my too susceptible sole filled up
agin; the teers started; but that vent wuznt enuff,
and I fell faintin onto the floor. Twenty or thirty
Northern delegates seed me fallin, and ketchin site
uv the gray coat, with the brass star onto it, rushed
to ketch me; and they bore me out uv the wigwam.
Sed one, " Wat a techin scene! overpowered by his
feelins." " Yes," sed another: " he deserves a
apintment."

I didn't go back to the Convenshun, coz I knowd
it wan't no yoose; and besides, after all the teers
that had been shed, — the members wringin their
handkerchers onto the floor, — it wuz sloppy under
foot. Conciliation and tenderness gushed out uv em.
I knowd it would be all right; it couldn't be otherwise. There wuz bonds wich held the members
together, and prevented the possibility uv trouble.
Johnson, hevin a ambition to head a party, must
hev a party to head. The Northern delegashun —
wich hed formerly actid with the Ablishnists —

couldn't do nothin without the Democracy North; and both on em combined couldn't do nothin without the Democracy South, The President cood depend on the Democracy North, coz he holds the offices; the Democracy North cood depend on the President, coz he must hev their votes. The President cood depend on the Democracy South, coz they want him to make a fight agin a Ablishen Congris, wich is a unconstooshnelly keepin uv em out, and preventin em from wollopin their niggers; the Democracy South cood depend on the President, coz he must hev their Representatives in their seats to beat the Ablishnists in Congris, — all cood depend on all, each cood depend on the other, coz each faction, or ruther each stripe, hed its little private axe to grind, wich it coodent do without the others to turn the grind-stone.

The Southern delegates, some on em, wuznt so well pleased. "What in thunder," sed one uv em, "did they mean by pilin on the agony over the the Yanks we killed? by pledgin us to give up the ijee uv seceshen, and by pledgin on us to pay the Nashnel Yankee debt?"

"'Sh!" sed I; "easy over the rough places. My friend, they didn't mean it; or, ef they did, *we* didn't. Is a oath so hard to break? Wood it

trouble that eminent patriot Breckenridge, after all
the times he swore to support the Constitution, to
sware to it wunst more? and wood it trouble him to
break it any more than it did in '61? Nay, verily.
Dismiss them gloomy thots. Vallandigham wuz
kicked out; but a thousand mules, and all uv em
old and experienced, cooden't kick him out uv our
service. Doolittle talked Northern talk, coz it's a
habit he got into doorin the war; but he'll git over
it. Raymond will be on our side this year, certain,
for last year he was agin us; and by the time he
is ready to turn agin, he'll be worn to so small a
pint that he won't be worth hevin; and the Democrisy uv the North wuz alluz ourn, and ef they wuzzent, the offices Johnson hez in reserve will draw
em like lode stun.

"My deer sir, I wunst knowd a Irishman, who
wuz sense killed in a Fenian raid, employed as a ar-
tist in well diggin. It wuz his lot to go to the bottom
uv the excavation and load the buckets with earth.
The dinner horn sounded, and he, with the alacrity
characteristic uv the race, sprang into the bucket,
and told em to hist away; and they histed. But ez
they histed, they amoozed themselves a droppin
earth onto him. 'Shtop!' sed he; but they didn't.
'Shtop!' sed he, 'or, be gorra! I'll cut the rope.'

My dear sir, Randall, and Doolittle, and Seward, and Johnson are a histin us out uv the pit we fell into in 1860. Their little talk about debts, and slavery, and sich, is the earth they're droppin onto us for fun; but shel we, like ijeots, cut the rope? Nary! Let em hist; and when we're safe out, and on solid ground, we kin, ef we desire, turn and chuck em into the hole."

All went off satisfied: the Northern men, for they carried home with em their commishuns; I, feelin that my Post office wuz sekoor; for ef, with the show we've got, we can't reëlect Johnson, the glory uv the Democracy hez departed indeed.

PETROLEUM V. NASBY, P. M.

(wich is Postmaster.)

XXX.

The Great Presidential Excursion to the Tomb of Douglas. — An Account of the Ride of the Modern John Gilpin, who went a Pleasuring and came Home with nothing but the Necks of His Bottles: by His Chaplain. — From Washington to Detroit.

AT THE BIDDLE HOUSE
(wich is in Detroit, Michigan),
September the 4th, 1866.

STEP by step I am assendin the ladder uv fame; step by step I am climbin to a proud eminence. Three weeks ago I wuz summoned to Washinton by that eminently grate and good man, Androo Johnson, to attend a consultation ez to the proposed Western tour, wich wuz to be undertaken for the purpose uv arousin the masses uv the West to a sence uv the danger wich wuz threatnin uv em in case they persisted in centralizin the power uv the Government into the hands uv a Congress, instid uv diffusin it throughout the hands uv one man, wich is Johnson. I got there too late to take part in the first uv the discussion. When I arrove they hed everything settled cepting the appintment uv a Chaplain for the excursion. The President insisted upon my fillin that position, but Seward objected. He wanted Beecher, but Johnson wuz inflexibly agin him. "I am determined," sez he, "to carry out my policy, but I hev some bowels left. Beecher hez done enuff already, considerin the pay he got. No, no! he shel be spared this trip; indeed he shel."

"Very good," said Seward; "but at least find some clergyman who endorses us without hevin P. M. to his honored name. It wood look better."

"I know it wood," replied Johnson; "but where kin we find sich a one? I hev swung around the entire circle, and heven't ez yet seen him. Nasby it must be."

There wuz then a lively discussion ez to the propriety, before the procession started, of removin all the Federal offis-holders on the proposed route, and appintin men who beleeved in us (Johnson, Beecher, and Me), that we might be shoor uv a sootable recepshun at each pint at wich we wuz to stop. The Annointed wuz in favor uv it. Sez he, "Them ez won't support my polisy shan't eat my bread and butter." Randall and Doolittle chimed in, for it's got to be a part of their religion to assent to whatever the President sez, but I mildly protested. I owe a duty to the party, and I am determined to do it.

"Most High," sez I, " a settin hen wich is lazy makes no fuss; cut its head off, and it flops about, for a while, lively. Lincoln's office-holders are settin hens. They don't like yoo nor yoor policy, but while they are on their nests, they will keep moderitly quiet. Cut off their heads, and they will spurt their blood in your face. Ez to bein enshoord of a reception at each point, you need fear nothin. Calkerlatin moderately, there are at least twenty-five or thirty patriots who feel a call for every offis in your disposal. So long, Yoor Highnis, ez them offisis is held just where they kin see em, and they don't know wich is to git em, yoo may depend upon the entire enthoosiasm uv each, individyooally and collectively. In short, ef there's 4 offises in a town, and yoo make the appointments, yoo hev sekoored 4 supporters; till yoo make the appointments yoo hev the hundred who expect to get em."

The President agreed with me that until after the trip the gullotine shood stop.

Secretary Seward sejested that a clean shirt wood improve my personal appearance, and akkordingly a cirkular wuz sent to the clerks in the Departments, assessin em for that purpose. Sich uv em ez refoosed to contribute their quota wuz instantly dismissed for disloyalty.

At last we started, and I must say we wuz got up in a highly conciliatory style. Every wun of the civilians uv the party wore buzzum pins, et settry, wich wuz presented to em by the Southern delegates to the Philadelphia Convention, wich wuz made uv the bones uv Federal soldiers wich hed fallen at various battles. Sum uv em were partiklerly valuable ez anteeks, hevin bin made from the bones uv the fust soldiers who fell at Bull Run.

The Noo York recepshun wuz a gay affair. I never saw His Imperial Highness in better spirits, and he delivered his speech to better advantage than I ever heard him do it before, and I bleeve I've heard it a hundred times. We left Noo York sadly. Even now, ez I write, the remembrance uv that perceshun, the recollection uv that banquet, lingers around me, and the taste uv them wines is still in my mouth. But we hed to go. We hed a mishn to perform, and we put ourselves on a steamboat and started.

ALBANY. — There wuz a immense crowd, but the Czar uv all the Amerikas didn't get orf his speech here. The Governor welcomed him, but he welcomed him ez the Cheef Magistrate uv the nashen, and happened to drop in Lincoln's name. That struck a chill over the party, and the President got out uv it ez soon ez possible. Bein reseeved ez Chief Magistrate, and not ez the great Pacificator, ain't His Eggslency's best holt. It wuz unkind uv Governor Fenton to do it. If he takes the papers, he must know that His Mightiness ain't got but one speech, and he ought to hev made sich a reception ez wood hev enabled him to hev got it off. We shook the dust off uv our feet, and left Albany in disgust.

SKENACTADY. — The people uv this delightfull little village wuz awake when the Imperial train arrived. The changes hadn't bin made in the offices here, and consekently there wuz a splendid recepshun. I didn't suppose there wuz so many patriots along the Mohawk. I wuz pinted out by sum one ez the President's private adviser — a sort uv private Secretary uv State ; and after the train started, I found jest 211 petitions for the Post Offis in Skenaktedy in my side coat pocket, wich the patriots who hed hurrahed so vociferously hed dexterously deposited there. The incident wuz a movin one. " Thank God!" thought I. " So long ez we hev

14

the post offices to give, we kin alluz hev a party.
The Sultan swung around the cirkle wunst here,
and leaving the Constooshun in their hands, the
train moved off.

UTICA. — The President spoke here with greater
warmth, and jerked more originality than I hed
before observed. He introdoost here the remark
that he didn't come to make a speech; that he wuz
goin to shed a tear over the tomb uv Douglas; that,
in swingin around the circle, he hed fought traitors
on all sides uv it, but that he felt safe. He shood
leave the Constooshn in their hands, and ef a martyr
wuz wanted, he wuz ready to die with neetness and
dispatch.

ROME. — Here we hed a splendid recepshun, and
I never heard His Majesty speek more felicitously.
He menshuned to the audience that he hed swung
around the Southern side uv the cirkle, and wuz
now swingin around the Northern side uv it, and
that he wuz fightin traitors on all sides. He left the
Constitooshun in their hands, and bid em good bye.
I received at this pint only 130 petitions for the post
office, wich I took ez a bad omen for the comin
election.

LOCKPORT. — The President is improvin wonder-
fully. He rises with the occasion. At this pint he

mentioned that he wuz sot on savin the country wich hed honored him. Ez for himself, his ambishn wuz more than satisfied. He hed bin Alderman, Member uv the Legislacher, Congressman, Senator, Military Governor, Vice-President, and President. He hed swung around the entire circle uv offises, and all he wanted now wuz to heal the wounds uv the nashen. He felt safe in leavin the Constooshn in their hands. Ez he swung around the cirkle —

At this pint I interrupted him. I told him that he hed swung around the cirkle wunst in this town, and ez yooseful ez the phrase wuz, it might spile by too much yoose.

At Cleveland we begun to get into hot water. Here is the post to which the devil uv Ablishnism is chained, and his chain is long enough to let him rage over neerly the whole State. I am pained to state that the President wuzn't treated here with the respeck due his station. He commenst deliverin his speech, but wuz made the subjeck uv ribald laffture. Skasely hed he got to the pint uv swingin around the cirkle, when a foul-mouthed nigger-lover yelled "Veto!" and another vocifferated "Noo Orleens!" and another remarked "Memphis!" and one after another interruption occurred until His Highness wuz completely turned off the track, and got wild.

He forgot his speech, and struck out crazy, but the starch wuz out uv him, and he wuz worsted. Grant, wich we hed taken along to draw the crowds, played dirt on us here, and stepped onto a boat for Detroit, leavin us only Farragut ez a attraction, who tried twice to git away ditto, but wuz timely prevented. The President recovered his ekanimity, and swung around the cirkle wunst, and leavin the Constooshn in their hands, retired.

At the next pint we wuz astounded at seein but one man at the station. He wuz dressed with a sash over his shoulder, and wuz wavin a flag with wun hand, firin a saloot with a revolver with the other, and playin "Hail to the Chief!" on a mouth organ, all to wunst.

"Who are you, my gentle friend?" sez I.

"I'm the newly-appinted Postmaster, sir," sez he. "I'm a perceshun a waitin here to do honor to our Cheef Magistrate, all alone, sir. There wuz twenty Johnsonians in this hamlet, sir; but when the commishn came for me, the other nineteen wuz soured, and sed they didn't care a d—n for him nor his policy, sir. Where is the President?"

Androo wuz a goin to swing around the cirkle for this one man, and leave the Constooshn in his hands, but Seward checked him.

At Fremont we hed a handsome recepshun, for the offises hevn't bin changed there, but Toledo didn't do so well. The crowd didn't cheer Androo much, but when Farragut was trotted out they gave him a rouser, wich wuz anything but pleasin to the Cheef Magistrate uv this nashen, who bleeves in bein respected.

Finally we reeched Detroit. This bein a Democratic city, the President wuz hisself agin. His speech here wuz wun uv rare merit. He gathered together in one quiver all the sparklin arrows he had used from Washington to this point, and shot em one by one. He swung around the cirkle; he didn't come to make a speech; he hed bin Alderman uv his native town; he mite hev been Dicktater, but woodent; and ended with a poetickal cotashun wich I coodent ketch, but wich, ez neer ez I cood understand, wuz, —

> "Kum wun, kum all; this rock shel fly
> From its firm base — in a pig's eye."

Here we repose for the nite. To-morrow we start onward, and shel continue swingin around the cirkle till we reach Chicago.

PETROLEUM V. NASBY, P. M.
(wich is Postmaster),
and likewise Chaplin to the expedishn.

XXXI.

The Presidential Tour Continued. —From Detroit
to Indianapolis.

POST OFFIS, CONFEDRIT X ROADS
(wich is in the Stait uv Kentucky),
September 11, 1866.

I AM at home, and glad am I that I am at home.
Here in Kentucky, surrounded by Dimicrats, im-
mersed a part of the time in my offishel dooties, and
the balance uv the time in whiskey, with the privilege uv wallopin niggers, and the more inestimable
and soothing privilege uv assistin in mobbin uv
Northern Ablishnists, who are not yet all out uv
the State, time passes pleasantly, and leaves no vain
regrets.   I alluz go to bed nites, feeling that the day
hez not bin wasted.

From Detroit the Presidential cavalcade, or ez
the infamous Jacobin Radical party irrevelently
term it, the menajery, proceeded to Chicago.   The
recepshuns his Imperial Highniss received through
Michigan were flatterin in the extreme.   I continue
my diary :

IPSLANTY. — At this pint the President displayed that originality and fertility uv imaginashun karacteristic uv him. The recepshun wuz grand. The masses called for Grant, and His Highness promptly responded. He asked em, ef he was Judis Iskariot who wuz the Saviour? Thad Stevens? If so, then after swingin around the cirkle, and findin traitors at both ends of the line, I leeve the 36 States with 36 stars onto em in yoor hands, and ——

The train wuz off amid loud shouts uv " Grant! Grant!" to wich the President responded by wavin his hat.

ANN ARBOR. — At this pint the train moved in to the inspiring sounds uv a band playin " Hale to the Cheef," and vocifrous cries uv " Grant! Grant!" His Majesty smilinly appeared and thanked em for the demonstration. It was soothin, he remarked. The air their band wuz playin, " Hail to the Chief," wuz appropit, ez he wuz Chief Magistrate uv the nashen, to wich posishen he hed reached, hevin bin Alderman uv his native village, U. S. Senator, etsettry. The crowd hollered " Grant! Grant!" and the President thanked em for the demonstration. It showed him that the people wuz with him in his efforts to close his eyes on a Union uv 36 States and a flag uv 36 stars onto it. Ef I am a traitor, sed he, warmin up, who is the Judis Iscariot? Ez I'm swingin around the cirkle, I find Thad Stevens on the one side and Jeff Davis on the ——

The conductor cruelly startid the train, without givin him time to finish.

The crowd proposed three cheers for Grant, and the President waved his hat to em, sayin that he thanked em, showing as it did that the people wuz with him.

BATTLE CREEK. — A large number was assembled here, who, ez the train stopped, yelled " Grant! Grant!" Affected to tears by the warmth uv the reception, the President thanked em for this mark of confidence. Ef he ever hed any doubts ez to the people's being with him, these doubts wuz removed. He wood leave in their hands the flag and the Union uv 36 States, and the stars thereto appertaining. Ef he wuz a Joodis Iskariot who wuz ——

The crowd gave three hearty cheers for Grant ez the train moved off, to wich the President responded by wavin his hat.

KALAMAZOO. — The offishels were on hand at this pint, and so wuz the people — 4 offishels and several thousand people, which the latter greeted us with cheers for Grant! Grant! The President responded, sayin, that in swingin around the cirkle, he hed bin called Joodis Iskariot for sacrificin uv hisself for the people! Who wuz the Saviour? Wuz Thad Stevens? No! Then cleerly into yoor hands I leave the Constitution uv 36 stars with 36 States onto em, intact and undissevered.

The offishels received the stars and States, and amid cheers for Grant, for which the President thanked em, the train glode off magestically.

And so on to Chicago, where we didn't get off our speech, though from the manner in wich the people hollered Grant! Grant! we felt cheered at realizin how much they wuz with us. His eminence wanted to sling the 36 States and the flag with the stars at em, but ez General Logan wuz there, ready to fling em back, it wuz deemed highly prudent not to do it.

Here my trials commenst. At the Biddle House, in Detroit, the nigger waiters showed how much a African kin be spiled by bein free. *They hed the impudence to refoose to wait on us,* and for a half hour the imperial stumick wuz forced to fast. This alarmin manifestation uv negro malignancy alarmed His Eggsalency. "Thank God!" sed he, "that I vetoed the Freedmen's Buroo Bill. I hev bin Alderman uv my native town — I hev swung around the entire cirkle, but this I never dreemed

uv. What would they do if they hed their rites?"
The insident made an impression onto him, and at
Chicago he resolved to trust em no longer. He
ordered his meals to his room, and sent for me.
"My friend," sed he, "taste evrything onto this
table."

"Why? my liege," sed I.

"Niggers is cooks," sed he, "and this food may
be pizoned. They hate me, for I ain't in the Moses
bizness. Taste, my friend."

"But spozn," sed I, "that it *shood* be pizoned?
Wat uv *my* bowels? My stomick is uv ez much
valyoo to me ez yourn is to yoo."

"Nasby," sez he, "taste! Ef yoo die, who
mourns? Ef I die, who'd swing around the cirkle?
Who'd sling the flag and the 36 stars at the people,
and who'd leave the Constooshn in their hands?
The country demands the sacrifice ; and besides, ef
yoo don't, off goes yoor offishl head."

That last appele fetched me. Ruther than risk
that offis I'd chaw striknine, for uv what akkount
is a Dimokrat, who hez wunst tasted the sweets
uv place, and is ousted? And from Chicago on I
wuz forced to taste his food and likker — to act
ez a sort uv a litenin-rod to shed off the vengeance
uv the nigger waiters. I wood taste uv every dish

and drink from each bottle, and ef I didn't swell up and bust in 15 minits His serene Highness wood take hold. I suffered several deaths. I resoom my diary:

JOLIET. — The crowd wuz immense. The peasantry, ez the train approached, rent the air with shouts uv " Grant!" " Grant!" His Potency, the President, promptly acknowledged the compliment. He was sacrificin hisself for them — who hed made greater sacrifices? He hed bin Alderman uv his native town, and Vice-President; he wuz too modest to make a speech; but ef he wuz Joodas Iskariot, who wuz the Saviour? He hed swung around the cirkle, and hedn't found none so far. He left in their hands the ——

And so on, until near St. Louis, when we penetrated a Democratic country, uv wich I informed his Majesty. " How knowest thou?" sez he. " Easy," sez I. " I observe in the crowds a large proportion uv red noses, and hats with the tops off. I notice the houses unpainted, with pig pens in front ov em; and what is more, I observe that crowds compliment yoo direct, instead of doin it, ez heretofore, over Grant's shoulders. The Knights uv the Golden Cirkle, wich I spect is the identical cirkle yoo've bin swingin around lately, love yoo and approach yoo confidently."

The President brisked up, and from this to Indianapolis he spoke with a flooidity I never observed in
him before. I may say, to yoose a medikle term,
that he had a hemorrhage uv words. At the latter
city our reception was the most flatrin uv eny we
have experienced. The people, when the President appeared on the balcony uv the Bates House,
yelled so vociferously for Grant, that the President,
when he stepped forward to acknowledge the
compliment, coodent be heard at all. He waved
his hat; and the more he waved it the more
complimentary the crowd became. " Grant! "
" Grant! " they yelled; and the more the President showed himself the more they yelled Grant,
until, overpowered by the warmth uv the recepshun,
and unwillin to expose his health, the President
retired without slingin a speech at em, but entirely
satisfied that the people wuz with him.

The next mornin the office-holders uv the State,
without the people, assembled, and he made his
regler speech to em, wich appeared to be gratifyin
to both him and them. The President does not like
to sleep with a undelivered speech on his mental
stumick. It gives him the nitemare.

Here I left the party, for a short time, that I mite
go home and attend to my official dooties. There is

five Northern families near the Corners wich must hev notice to leave, and eight niggers to hang.   I hed orders to report to the party somewhere between Looisville and Harrisburgh, wich I shall do, ez, travelin by order, I get mileage and sich.

Petroleum V. Nasby, P. M.

(wich is Postmaster,)

and likewise Chaplin to the expedishn.

XXXII.

The End of the Presidential Tour.— From Louisville to Washington.

WHITE HOUSE, WASHINGTON, D. C., }
September, 12, '66. }

I REJINED the Presidenshel party at Looisville, and glad I am that I did it at that pint. His Imperial Serenity hed bin pleased ever sence he left Chicago, or rather sence he got near St. Loois, for two-thirds uv Illinois wuz pizen, and Indianapolis wuz pizener. From St. Loois the recepshuns wuz trooly corjel and even enthoosiastic. We got out uv the region uv aristocrats, and hed come down to the hard-fisted yomanry. I seed holes thro the hats uv men ; I seed wat mite be called the flag uv Democrisy wavin from behind em, which, ez they genrally either had no coats at all, or if any, they were roundabouts, wuz alluz in view. I saw wimen who disdained stockins and dipped snuff, and I felt to home. I wuz among Democracy. The cheerin for Grant and Farragut closed ez we got into them regions, and uv the vociferous crowds half uv em, the younger ones, cheered Andrew Johnson, while the old veterans, them whose noses wuz blossomin for the tomb, cheered for Andrew Jackson. His Serenity smilinly acknowledged both, by makin a speech to em, and wavin his hat.

With these preliminary remarks I resoom my diary : —

Louisville. — There wuz a magnificent demonstration here. His Imperial Majesty, who wuz in a eggslent condition to make crowds large enough, remarked to me as we wuz ridin through the streets : " 'Splen 'splay ! 'Mor'n ten 'unerd sousand people — mor'n ten million people — mor'n ten 'unerd million people — mor'n ten 'unerd sousand million people — and alluvum 'sporters my policy. ' Rah for me ! "

His Majesty ondoubtedly eggsagerated towards the last ; but it is safe to put the throng down at a good many. That estimate is entirely safe. There wuz the finest display uv banners and sich I hev seen since we startid. The red white and red wuz displayed from almost half the houses, ladies waved their handkerchiefs ez we passed, and men cheered. A pleasin incident occurd here. I noticed one gushin maiden uv thirty-seven wavin her handkercher ez tho she was gettin so much per wave, and had rent to pay that nite. I recognized her to wunst. When I wuz a citizen uv Ohio, and wuz drafted into the service uv the United States, and clothed in a bob-tailed blue coat, and hed a Oystran muskit put into my unwillin hands, and forced to fite agin my brethren, our regiment passed thro Looisville and stayed there some days. I wuz walkin one after-noon, when I met this identical angel. She saw my bloo kote, and enraged, spit in my face with sich energy that she threw out uv her mouth a full sett uv false teeth. I returned em gallantly, wiped my face with my handkercher, and vowed that hand-kercher shood henceforth be kept sacred. It wuz; and when I seed her wavin hern at our party, I wept like a Philadelphia Convenshen. I stopped the carriage, met the patriotic female, called her attention to the incident, and handed her my hand-kercher which hed, four years before, wiped her spittle. The incident gave new vigor to her arms, and from that time she waved two handkerchers, and mine wuz one uv em. I narrated the insident to the President, and he wept.

There wuz a large perceshen and a great variety of banners. Among the most noticeable, wuz a company uv solgers uv the late war, each with a leg off, dressed in the gray uniforms into wich they hed been mustered out, with this motto: "We are willin to go the other leg for A. Jonson." Another company uv solgers, who hed each lost an arm, carried this inscription: "What we didn't get by bullets, we shel get by ballots."

The President cut down his speech jest one half here. In swingin around the cirkle he omitted to menshen that he found traitors on the Southern side uv it. But he left the constooshn in their hands cheerfully.

CINCINNATI. — A very enthoosiastic recepshen — continyood and loud cheers for Grant, wich the President acknowledged. A unsophisticated Postmaster, who jined us here, wanted to know why the people cheered for Grant instid uv the President, to which His Highness answered that they wuz considrit — they knew his modesty, and wanted to spare his blushes. Another man, who wuz also unsophisticated, asked him, confidenshelly, ef he didn't think there wuz a samenis in his speeches, and that ef he didn't think he'd do better to give a greater variety. His Eggslency asked him how there *cood* be more variety. "At Cincinnati," sed he, "I observed the followin order: —

15

1. I swung around the cirkle.

2. I asked who wuz the Saviour ef I wuz Joodis Iskariot?

3. I left the Constitooshn, the 36 States, and the flag with 36 stars onto it, in their hands.

Now, at Columbus, I shel vary it thusly :

1. The Constitooshn, flag, and stars.

2. The Joodis Iskariot biznis.

3. Swingin around the cirkle.

At Stoobenville, agin, ez follows :

1. Joodis Iskariot.

2. Swingin around the cirkle.

3. Constitooshn, flag, and stars.

And so on. It's susceptible uv many changes. I thot uv that when I writ that speech, and divided it up into sections on purpose."

JOHNSTOWN, PA. — A bridge fell down, onto wich wuz 400 voters, killin a dozen uv em. His Eggslency felt releeved when heerin uv the axident, at bein asshoored that there wuzn't wun uv his supporters on the bridge. He considered it a speshl Providence. The condukter overheerd the remark, and answered, that ef any uv his supporters wuz killed in that seckshun they'd have to import wun for the purpose.

MIFFLIN, PA. — A enthoosiastic indivijjle who

wants the Post Office at this place very much, fell on the President's neck, and wept, hailin him ez the " Preserver uv the Union." The President thanked him for this spontaneous triboot, and left in his hands the Constitooshun, the flag, and the appintment he desired.

BALTIMORE. — There wuz a spontaneous recepshun here, wich wuz gratifying to us. The perceshun wuz immense, and the mottoes expressive. One division wuz headed by the identikle indivijooel who fired the first shot at the Massachusetts men in 1861. He is a ardent supporter uv President Johnson's policy. One flag wuz capchered from a Injeany regiment at the first Bull Run, at wich the President wept. " Things is becomin normal," sed he, " when the people will stand that. Wat love ! — wat unity ! The flags uv both secshuns, wich was lately borne by foes, now minglin in the same proceshun, and all uv em cheerin ME."

At last we arrived at Washinton, hevin swung entirely round the cirkle, and found traitors North and South. The demonstrashen to greet the President on his arrival was immense. The clerks in all the departments wuz out (at least them ez wuzn't will wish they hed bin, ez their names wuz all taken), the solgers on duty wuz ordered out, and

altogether it wuz the most spontaneous exhibition
I ever witnest. The Mayor made a speech. The
President asked if he was Joodis Iscariot who wuz
the Saviour — told him he had swung around the
entire cirkle, and hed found traitors on all sides uv
it, though sence he left Cleveland, Chicago, and
Indianapolis he wuz satisfied there wuz the heft uv
them in the North; but be this ez it may, he left
the Constooshn, and the 36 States, and the flag
with 36 stars onto it, in his hands. He had bin
Alderman uv his native village, and Congressman,
and United States Senator, and Vice-President, and
President, wich latter circumstance he considered
forchinit, but wuz, after all, an Humble Indivij'le.
He didn't feel his oats much, and wood do his dooty
agin traitors North, ez well as agin his misguided
friends South.

And so ended the Presidential excursion.

PETROLEUM V. NASBY, P. M.
(wich is Postmaster),
and likewise Chaplin to the expedishn.

P. S.   I forgot to menshun that at Chicago we
laid the corner-stone uv a monument to Douglas.
The occurence hed entirely slipped my memory.

P. V. N.

XXXIII.

At Home again. — A detailed Account of Soul-harrowing Outrages inflicted upon the People of Confederate × Roads by a Party of Freedmen, and how the Insult was wiped out.

POST OFFIS, CONFEDRIT × ROADS
(wich is in the Stait uv Kentucky),
September 16, 1866.

I FOUND my flock in a terrible state uv depression, at which, when I wuz told the cause, I didn't wonder at. There wuz, back of the Corners on the side hill, over towards Garrettstown, about three quarters uv a mile this side of Abbott's grocery (we estimate distance here from one grocery to another), five or six families uv niggers. The males of this settlement had all been in the Federal army ez soljers, and hed saved their pay, and bounty, and sich, and hed bought uv a disgustid Confederate, who proposed to find in Mexico that freedom which was denied him here, and who, bein determined to leave the country, didn't care who he sold his plantashen to, so ez he got greenbax, three hundred acres, wich they hed divided up, and built cabins onto em, and wuz a cultivatin it. There wuz a store-keeper at the Corners who come here from Illinoy, and who hed been so greedy uv gain and so graspin ez to buy their prodoose uv em, and sell em sich supplies ez they needed. These accursed sons and daughters of Ham was a livin there in comfort. The thing was a gittin unendoorable. They come to the Corners dressed in clothes without patches, and white shirts, and hats on; and the females in dresses, and hoops under em; in short, these apes hed assoomed so much uv the style uv people that ef it hadn't bin for their black faces, they wood have passed for folks.

Our people become indignant, and ez soon ez I returned, I was requested to call a meetin to consider the matter, which I uv course did.

The horn wuz tootid, and the entire Corners wuz assembled, eggscepting the Illinoy store-keeper, who didn't attend to us much. I stated briefly and elokently (I hev improved in public speakin sense I heered His Serene Highness, Androo the I., all the way from Washinton to Looisville), and asked the brethren to ease their minds.

Squire Gavitt hed observed the progress uv them

niggers with the most profoundest alarm. He hed noticed em comin to the Corners, dressed better nor his family dressed, and sellin the produx uv their land to that wretch —

At this point the Illinoy store-keeper come in, and the Squire proceeded.

— he shood say Mr. Pollock, and he hed made inquiries, and found that one family hed sold three hundred and seventy-five dollars worth uv truck, this season, uv which they hed laid out for clothes and books two hundred dollars, leavin em one hundred and seventy-five dollars in cash, which was more money than he hed made sense the accursed Linkin passed the emancipashen proclamation. And what hed driv the iron into his soul wuz the fact that wun of them niggers wuz *his* nigger. " The money they hev," pursood the Squire, " is MY MONEY ; that man worth $1500 is my man ; his wife is my woman ; her children my children — "

" That's a literal fact !" shouted Joe Bigler, a drunken, returned Confederate sojer ; " they hev yoor nose eggsactly, and they're the meanest yaller brats in the settlement."

This unhappy remark endid in a slite unpleasantness, wich resultid in the Squire's bein carried out, minus one ear, and his nose smashed. Joseph

remarked that he'd wantid to git at him ever sense
he woodn't lend him a half dollar two months ago.
He was now satisfied, and hoped this little episode
woodn't mar the harmony uv the meetin.

Elder Smathers observed that he hed noticed
with pain that them niggers alluz hed money, and
wuz alluz dresst well, while we, their sooperiors,
hed no money, and nothin to boast uv in the way uv
close.   He wood say —

Pollock, the Illinoy store-keeper, put in.   Ef the
Elder wood work ez them niggers wuz workin, and
not loaf over half the time at Bascom's grocery, he
mite possibly hev a hull soot uv close, and now and
then a dollar in money.   It wuz here, ez it wuz in
all strikly Dimekratic communities, the grocery
keepers absorb all the floatin capital, and —

He wuz not allowed to proceed.   Bascom flung
a chair at him, and four or five uv his constitooents
fell on him.   He wuz carried out for dead.   Bascom
remarked that he wuz for the utmost freedom uv
speech, but in the discussion uv a grate Constooshnel
question, no Illinoy Ablishnist shood put in his
yawp.   The patriotic remark wuz cheered, but
when Bascom ask't the whole meetin out to drink,
the applause wuz uproarious.   Bascom alluz gets
applause ; he knows how to move an audience.

Deekin Pogram sed he'd bore with them niggers till his patience wuz gin out. He endoored it till last Sunday. After service he felt pensive, ruther, and walked out towards Garrettstown, meditatin, as he went, on the sermon he hed listened to that mornin on the necessity uv the spread of the Gospil. Mournin in sperit over the condition of the heathen, he didn't notis where he wuz till he found hisself in the nigger settlement, and in front uv one uv their houses. There he saw a site wich paralyzed him. There wuz a nigger, wich wuz wunst his nigger, wich Linkin deprived him uv, settin under his porch, and a profanin the Holy Bible by teachin his child to read it! "Kin this be endoored?" the Deekin asked.

Deekin Parkins sed he must bear his unworthy testimony agin these disturbers. They hed — he knowd whereof he spoke — hired a female woman from Massachusetts to teach their children! He hed bin in their skool-room, and with his own eyes witnest it.

Bascom, the grocery keeper, hed bin shocked at their conduct. He wuz convinct that a nigger wuz a beast. They come to the Corners to sell the produx of their lands; do they leave their money at his bar? Nary! They spend sum uv it at the store uv a disorganizer from Illinoy, who is here interferin with the biznis uv troo Southern men, but he hed never seed one uv em inside his door. He hed no pashence with em, and believed suthin shood be done to rid the community uv sich yooseless inhabitance. Ef they ever git votes they'r agin us. No man who dodges my bar ever votes straight Dimocrisy.

Ginral Punt moved that this meetin do to wunst proceed to the settlement, and clean em out. They wuz a reproach to Kentucky. Of course, ez they were heathens and savages, sich goods ez they hed wood fall to the righteous, uv whom we wuz which, and he insisted upon a fair divide. All he wanted wuz a bureau and a set uv chairs he hed seen.

The motion wuz amendid to inclood Pollock, the Illinoy store-keeper, and it wuz to wunst acted upon.

Pollock wuz reconstructed first. Filled with zeal for the right, his door wuz bustid in, and in a jiffy the goods wich he wuz a contaminatin our people with wuz distributed among the people, each takin sich ez sooted em. Wun man sejested that ez they wuz made by Yankees, and brought south by Yankees, that there wuz contaminashen in the touch uv em, and that they be burned, but he wuz hooted down, our people seein a distinction. The contaminashen wuz in payin for em ; gittin em gratooitusly took the cuss off.

Elated, the crowd started for the settlement. I never saw more zeal manifested. A half hour brought us there, and then a scene ensood wich filled me with joy onspeekable. The niggers wuz routed out, and their goods wuz bundled after em. The Bibles and skool books wuz destroyed first, coz we hed no use for them ; their chairs, tables, and bureaus, clothin and beddin, wuz distributed. A wooman hed the impudence to beg for suthin she fancied, when the righteous zeal uv my next door neighbor, Pettus, biled over, and he struck her. Her husband, forgettin his color, struck Pettus, and the outrage wuz completed. *A nigger hed raised his hand agin a white man!*

The insulted Caucashen blood riz, and in less than a minit the bodies uv six male Ethiopians wuz a danglin in the air, and the bodies uv six Ethiopian wimin wuz layin prostrate on the earth. The children wuz spared, for they wuz still young, and not hevin bin taught to read so far that they could not forgit it, ef kept carefully from books, they kin be brought up in their proper speer, ez servance to their brethern. (By the way, the inspired writer must hev yoosed this word " brethern," in this connection, figeratively. The nigger, bein a beast, cannot be our brother.) Some may censure us for too much zeal in this matter, but what else cood we hev dun? We are high toned, and can't stand everything. These niggers hed no rite to irritate us by their presence. They knowd our feelins on the subjick, and by buyin land and remainin in the visinity, they kindled the flame wich resulted ez it did. Ez they did in Memphis and Noo Orleans, they brought their fate onto their own heads.

Pollock recovered, and with the Yankee school marm who wuz a teechin the niggers, left for the North yesterday. It speeks well for the forbearance uv our people that they wuz permitted to depart at all.

PETROLEUM V. NASBY, P. M.
(wich is Postmaster),
and likewise late Chaplin to the expedishn.

XXXIV.

*Is requested to act as Chaplain of the Cleveland
Convention. — That Beautiful City visited for
that Purpose.*

Post Offis, Confedrit × Roads
(wich is in the Stait uv Kentucky),
September 20, 1866.

I WUZ sent for to come to Washington, from my
comfortable quarters at the Post Offis, to attend
the convenshun uv sich soldiers and sailors uv the
United States ez bleeve in a Union uv 36 States,
and who hev sworn allejinse to a flag with 36 stars
onto it, at Cleveland.   My esteemed and life-long
friend and co-laborer, Rev. Henry Ward Beecher, wuz to hev bin the chaplin uv the convenshun,
but he failed us, and it wuz decided in a Cabinet
meetin that I shood take his place.   I didn't see the
necessity uv hevin a chaplin at every little convenshun uv our party, and so stated; but Seward remarked, with a groan, that ef ever there wuz a
party, since parties wuz invented, wich needed

prayin for, ours wuz that party. "And, Parson," sed he, glancin at a list uv delegates, "ef yoo hev any agonizin petitions, any prayers uv extra fervency, offer em up for these fellers. Ef there is any efficacy in prayer, it's my honest, unbiased opinion that there never wuz in the history uv the world, nor never will be agin, sich a magnificent chance to make it manifest. Try yoorself particularly on Custer; tho', after all," continyood he, in a musin, abstracted sort uv a way, wich he's fallen into lately, "the fellow is sich a triflin bein, that he reely kin hardly be held 'sponsible for what he's doin; and the balance uv em, good Hevens! they'r mostly druv to it by hunger." And the Secretary maundered on suthin about "sixty days" and "ninety days," paying no more attention to the rest uv us than ez ef we wuzn't there at all.

So, receevin transportashen and suffishent money from the secret service fund for expenses, I departed for Cleveland, and after a tejus trip thro' an Ablishn country, I arrived there. My thots were gloomy beyond expression. I hed recently gone through this same country ez chaplin to the Presidential tour, and every stashen hed its pecooliar onpleasant remembrances. Here wuz where the cheers for Grant were vociferous, with nary a snort

for His Eggslency; there wuz where the peasantry
laft in his face when he went thro' with the regler
ritooal uv presentin the constitooshn and the flag
with 36 stars onto it to a deestrick assessor; there
wuz — but why recount my sufferins? Why harrow
up the public bosom, or lasserate the public mind?
Suffice to say, I endoored it; suffice to say that I
hed strength left to ride up Bank street, in Cleveland, the seen uv the most awful insult the Eggsec-
utive ever receeved.

The evenin I arrived, the delegates, sich ez wuz
on hand, held a informal meetin to arrange matters
so ez they wood work smooth when the crowd
finally got together. Genral Wool wuz ez gay and
frisky ez though he reely belonged to the last giner-
ashn. There wuz Custar, uv Michigan, with his
hair freshly oiled and curled, and busslin about ez
though he hed cheated hisself into the beleef that
he reely amounted to suthin; and there wuz seventy-
eight other men, who hed distinguished theirselves
in the late war, but who hed never got their deserts,
ceptin by brevet, owin to the fact that the Adminis-
trashn wuz Ablishn, which they wuzn't. They were,
in a pekuniary pint uv view, suthin the worse for
wear, tho' why that shood hev bin the case I coodent
see (they hevin bin, to an alarmin extent, quarter-

masters and commissaries, and in the recrootin service), til I notist the prevailin color uv their noses,
and heerd one uv em ask his neighbor ef Cleveland
wuz blest with a faro bank! Then I knowd all
about it.

There wuz another pekooliarity about it which
for a time amoozed me. Them ez wuz present
wuz divided into 2 classes — those ez hed bin recently appinted to posishens, and them ez expected
to be shortly. I notist on the countenances uv the
first class a look uv releef, sich ez I hev seen in fac-
tories Saturday nite, after the hands wuz paid off
for a hard week's work; and on the other class the
most wolfish, hungry, fierce expression I hev ever
witnessed. Likewise, I notist that the latter set
uv patriots talked more hefty uv the necessity uv
sustainin the policy uv our firm and noble President,
and damned the Ablishunists with more emphasis
and fervency than the others.

One enthoosiastic individual, who hed bin quar-
termaster two years, and hed bin allowed to resign
"jest after the battle, mother," wich, hevin his papers all destroyed, made settlin with the government
a easy matter, wuz so feroshus that I felt called
upon to check him. "Gently, my frend," sed I,
"gently! I hev bin thro' this thing; I hev my

commission. It broke out on me jest ez it hez on yoo; but yoo won't git yoor Assessorship a minit sooner for it."

" It ain't a Assessorship I want," sez he. " I hev devoted myself to the task uv bindin up the wounds uv my beloved country —— "

" Did you stop anybody very much from inflictin them sed wounds?" murmured I.

" An ef I accept the Post Orfis in my native village, — which I hev bin solissited so strongly to take that I hev finally yielded, — I do it only that I may devote my few remainin energies wholly to the great cause uv restorin the 36 States to their normal posishens under the flag with 36 stars onto it, in spite uv the Joodis Iskariots wich, ef I am whom, wat is the Saviour, and — and where is —— "

Perseevin that the unfortunate man hed got into the middle uv a quotashen from the speech uv our noble and patriotic President, and knowin his intellek wuzn't hefty enough to git it off jist as it wuz originally delivered, I took him by the throat, and shet off the flood uv his elokence.

" Be quiet, yoo idiot!" remarked I, soothingly, to him. " Yoo'll git your apintment, becoz, for the fust time in the history uv this or any other Repub-

16

lic, there's a market for jist sich men ez yoo; but all this blather won't fetch it a minit sooner."

"Good Lord!" tho't I, ez I turned away, "wat a President A. J. is, to hev to buy up *sich* cattle! Wat a postmaster he must be, whose gineral cussedness turns *my* stummick!"

It wuz deemed necessary to see uv wat we wuz compozed; whereupon Kernel K——, who is now Collector uv Revenue in Illinoy, asked ef there wuz ary man in the room who hed bin a prizner doorin the late fratricidle struggle. A gentleman uv, perhaps, thirty aroze, and sed he wuz. He hed bin taken three times, and wuz, altogether, 18 months in doorance vile in three diffrent prizns.

Custar fell on his neck, and asked him, aggitatidly, ef he wuz shoor — quite shoor, after sufferin all that, that he supported the policy of the President? Are you quite shoor — quite shoor?

"I am," returned the phenomenon. "I stand by Andrew Johnson and his policy, and I don't want no office!!"

"Hev yoo got wun?" shouted they all in korus.

"Nary!" sed he. "With me it is a matter uv principle!"

"Wat prizns wuz yoo incarcerated in?" asked I, lookin at him with wonder.

" Fust at Camp Morton, then at Camp Douglas, and finally at Johnson's Island ! "

Custar dropt him, and the rest remarked that, while they hed a very helthy opinion uv him, they guessed he'd better not menshen his presence, or consider hisself a delegate. Ez ginerous foes they loved him ruther better than a brother; yet, as the call didn't quite inclood him, tho' there wuz a delightful oneness between em, yet, ef 'twuz all the same, he hed better not announce hisself. He wuz from Kentucky, I afterwards ascertained.

The next mornin, suthin over two hundred more arriv; and the delegashens bein all in, it wuz decided to go on with the show. A big tent hed bin brought on from Boston to accommodate the expected crowd, and quite an animated discussion arose ez to wich corner uv it the Convenshun wuz to ockepy. This settled, the biznis-wuz begun. Genral WOOL wuz made temporary Chairman, to wich honor he responded in a elokent extemporaneous speech, which he read from manuscript. General EWING made another extemporaneous address, which he read from manuscript, and we adjourned for dinner.

The dinner hour was spent in caucussin privately in one uv the parlors uv the hotel. The Chairman

asked who shood make speeches after dinner, wen
every man uv em pulled from his right side coat
pocket a roll uv manuscript, and sed he hed dotted
down a few ijees wich he hed conclooded to present
extemporaneously to the Convenshun.   That Babel
over, the Chairman sed he presoomed some one
shood be selected to prepare a address ; whereupon
every delegate rose, and pulled a roll uv manuscript
from his left side coat pocket, and sed he hed dotted
down a few ijees on the situashn, wich he proposed
to present, et settry.   This occasioned another
shindy ; wen the Chairman remarked " Resolu-
shens," wen every delegate rose, pulled a roll uv
manuscript from his right breast coat pocket, and
sed he hed jotted down a few ijees, wich, &c.

I stood it until some one mentioned me ez Chaplin to the expedition West, when the pressure becum
unendurable.   They sposed I was keeper uv the
President's conscience, and I hed not a minit's
peece after that.   In vain I ashoored em that, there
bein no consciences about the White House, no
one could hold sich a offis ; in vain I ashoored em
that I hed no influence with His Majesty.   Two
thirds uv em pulled applicashens for places they
wanted from the left breast coat pocket, and insistid
on my takin em, and seein that they was appinted.

THE CLEVELAND CONVENTION. Page 244.

I told em that I cood do nuthin for em ; but they
laft me to skorn. " You are jist the style uv man,"
said they, " who hez inflooence with His Eggslency,
and yoo must do it." Hemmed in, there wuz but
one way uv escape, and that way I took. Seezin a
carpet sack, wich, by the way, belonged to a delegate (I took it to give myself the look of a traveler),
I rushed to the depot, and startid home, entirely satisfied that ef Cleveland may be taken as a sample,
the less His Majesty depends on soljers, the better.

PETROLEUM V. NASBY, P. M.

(wich is Postmaster),

and likewise late Chaplin to the expedishn.

P. S. I opened the carpet sack on the train,
spectin to find a clean shirt in it, at least. It con-
tained, to my disgust, an address to be read before
the Cleveland Convention, a set uv resolutions, a
speech, and a petition uv the proprietor thereof for a
collectorship, signed by eight hundred names, and a
copy uv the Indiana State Directory for 1864. The
names wuz in one hand-writin, and wuz arranged
alphabetically.

XXXV.

An Appeal to the People just before the October Elections.

POST OFFIS, CONFEDRIT X ROADS
(wich is in the Stait uv Kentucky),
October 1, 1866.

PRESIDENT JOHNSON, who hez bin likened to Androo Jaxon, and wich, since my appintment I conseed him to be, in many partikelers, his sooperior, requested me and William H. Seward (his secretary and chaplin) to draw up and publish to the Democracy of the various States holdin elecshuns this fall an address, or ruther an appeal, firmly beleevin that hed he extendid his tour to Maine, and isshood an address to em, that that state wood not hev gone ez it did. William refoozed to take part in the appeal, sayin that it warnt uv no use, and so the dooty devolved upon me.

DEMOCRATS AND CONSERVATIVES UV THE NORTH:

Appresheatin the gravity uv the isshoo, I address yoo. The signs uv the times is ominus.

A Radikle Congress, electid durin the time when
the Southin States, wich comprises reely all the
intellek uv this people, didn't take no part in the
elekshen, bein too bizzy gettin out uv Sherman's
way to open polls, — a Congress, I repeat, in wich
there ain't no Southern man, and wich consekently
kant, by any stretch uv the hooman imaginashen, be
considered Constitooshnel, hez dared to thwart the
President uv the United States, and set up its will
agin hisn! I need skarcely recount its high-handed
acts uv usurpashen. It passed a bill givin rites to
niggers, wich, accordin to Scripter (see Onesimus,
Ham, and Hagar, the only three texts in Scripter
uv any partikeler account) and the yoosages uv the
Democrisy, ain't got no rites; and the President,
exercisin the high prerogatives put into his hands
by the Constitooshen, vetoed it. Here the matter
should hev endid. He hed expressed, in a manner
strikly Constitooshenel, his objecshens to the measure; and a proper regard for his feelins, and just
deference for his opinions, ought to hev indicated
the right course. Here wuz peace offered this Congres. Here wuz the tender uv a olive branch. The
President didn't want a quarrel with Congres; he
didn't desire a continyooance uv the agitation wich
hed shook the country like a Illinois ager; but he

desired Peece. Congres cood hev hed it hed they only withdrawed their crood noshens uv what wus rite and what wuz wrong; ratified, ez they shood hev done, sich laws ez the President saw fit to make : in short, hed they follered the correct rool when we hev a Demokratic President, and put the Government in his hands, with an abidin trust in his rectitood and wisdom, we mite hev avoided this struggle, and thus wood hev bin peaceful. But this reckless Congris, bent upon consentrating power in its hands instid uv dividin it between him and Sew-.ard, passed the bill over his head, regardlis uv his feelins ! The responsibility for the dissension rests, therefore, with Congres.

But these questions are altogether too hefty for the Demokratic intellek, and I fling em out for the considerashen uv the few Post Masters we get from the Union ranks. To the Dimocrisy I address my-self more partickerlerly.

Do you want to Marry a Nigger? This ishoo is agin before yoo. Are you in favor uv ele-vatin the Afrikin to a posishen where he kin be yoor ekal, or perhaps yoor sooperior? That ishoo is agin before yoo for yoor decision, only the danger to yoo is increased. The matter has become threat-ening ; for, disgise it ez we may, thousands uv em kin read, and they are akkumulatin property, and wearin good clothes to a extent trooly alarmin to the Dimokratic mind. We hev alluz consoled ourselves with the soothin reflection that there wuz a race lower down in the scale uv humanity than us uns. Shall we continue to enjoy that comfort? That's the question for every Dimokrat to consider when he votes this fall. Remove the weight uv legal disability, and ten to one ef they don't outstrip us even, and then where are we goin to look for a race to look down upon? It's a close thing atween us now ; and ez we uv this generation can't elevate ourselves, why, for our own peece uv mind, we must, — I repeet it, — MUST pull them down.

Agin then I repeet, Do you want to Marry a Nigger? Yoor daughters wunst carried banners onto wich wuz inskribed that trooly Dimokratic motto, "White husbands or none !" and in consequence they've bin mostly livin in the enjoyment uv none. Are they to go back on that holy determinashen to preserve the Anglo Sackson race on this continent in its purity? Do yoo want the nigger — the big buck nigger — the flat-footed nigger — the woolly-headed nigger — the long-heeled nigger — the bow-legged nigger — the Nigger — to step up aside uv yoo, and exercise the prerogatives uv freemen in this country? Do you want the nigger aforesed to be mayors uv your towns, with all the hatred they hev towards us? Wat chance, O Dimokratic dweller in cities! think yoo yoo'd hev if hauled up afore a nigger mayor on a charge uv disorderly conduct? Wat chance wood yoor children hev in a skool uv wich all the teechers wuz niggers? Wat chance wood yoo hev wen arrestid for small misdemeanors, afore nigger judges?

How, let me ask, in the name of High Heaven, wood yoo like to be tried for hoss stealin afore a nigger jury?

"But," say some uv yoo, who, set ravin by drums, and flags, and sich, went off violently into the war, and wuz, perhaps, saved from starvin by niggers, "these niggers wuz our friends in the late war — they fought agin the South!"

O, wat a deloosion! O, wat blindnis! Troo, they did; and that shows the danger that's afore us; that lifts the fog from the precipise onto wich we are standin, and shows us our danger. Wat does this fact prove? It proves the onreasonableness uv the Nigger — his discontentednis with the posishen to wich nacher assigned him, and his cussid disposition to upset the normal condition. The Bible makes him a servant unto his brethren (see

Ham, Hagar, and Onesimus, three blessed texts).
Science proves him to be, not a man, but a beast;
and so, take him ez we may, either ez our brother
or ez a beast, — and Dimocrisy, with that liberality
wich hez always distinguished it, gives every man
his choice wich theory to take, — his condition is
servitood. But he, with a cussidness, a perversity
wich I never cood understand, flies into the face uv
the Divine decree, flies into the face uv science, and
asserts his independence! He turned agin them ez
hed fostered him; turned agin, in many instances,
his own parents (in these instances, for convenience,
the parents adopted the brethren theory), and for
an abstract idea fought agin em. That restlessness
under bonds alarmed the Dimocratic mind. We
who owned em under the Skripter (see Onesimus,
Hagar, and Ham), and under the eternal laws uv
scientific trooth wuz content with the arrangement,
and why shood they not hev bin? Things wuz
normal. They worked, and we eat; and ef they
hed bin content with this ekitable division uv the
labor uv life, all wood hev bin smooth to-day.

Their takin part agin us at the South, and in
favor uv the Federals, is, instead uv a coz uv feelin
good toward em, a source uv oneasiness; instid uv
bein a reason for elevatin uv em, it's my principal

reason for depressin uv em. Sich onsettled minds
shood be quieted; this itchin to raise theirselves
shood be crushed out uv em, that Science and Holy
Writ (see Onesimus, Hagar, and Ham) may be
vindicated.

Shel we desert Androo Johnson, after all the
trouble he hez bin to in gettin back to us? Shel
we elect a Congres this fall so soaked in Ablishin —
so filled with objeckshuns to our Southern brethren,
ez to refooze to receive em back into the seats which
they vacated? Consider! The Southern Dimok-
racy hevn't, and don't, lay up nothin agin yoo.
They are willin to forgive and forget. They failed,
but they are willin to forgiv the cause uv the failyoor. They hevn't got the government they wanted, but they find no fault with that, but are willin to
take charge of the wun they hev bin compelled to
live under. Kin they offer fairer? The fate uv war
wuz agin em. Buryin all hard feelins, they extend
to us Chrischen charity, and say, Here we are —
take us — give us our old places. They hev bin
chastened. Their household gods hev bin destroyed, and their temples torn down. Wun neighbor uv mine lost two sons in the Confedrit army; another son, which he hed refoosed $1500 for in 1860,
he wuz compelled to shoot, coz he wuz bound to

run away into the Federal army; and two octoroons, which he hed a dozen times refoosed $2500
for, each, in Noo Orleans, he saw layin dead on
the steps uv a skool house in Memphis.   Hez he
suffered nothin?   And yet he is willin to take a seat
in Congress — forgettin all he hez suffered, and for-
givin the cause thereof.   What wickedness it is
wich would further bruise sich a broken reed!

Therefore, ez yoo love yourselves and hate the
nigger, I implore yoo to act.   Take yoor choice uv
the platforms uv the different States — vote ez a
Johnson Unionist, or ez a Democratic Johnsonian
— but vote.

Kentucky holds out her hands appealingly!   Kentucky implores yoo to bild up a bulwark North uv
the Ohio River to save what little is left uv pure
Dimocracy there!   Kentucky will back yoo in yoor
endeavors.   Will you heed her cry?   Shel she ap-
peel in vain?   Forbid it, Hevin!

PETROLEUM V. NASBY, P. M.
(wich is Postmaster).

XXXVI.

The October Elections. — The Effect the Result produced in Kentucky.

CONFEDRIT X ROADS
(wich is in the Stait uv Kentucky),
October 14, 1866.

THERE is mournin in Kentucky. The results of the elections in Ohio, Injeany, Pennsylvany, and Iowa reached me yesterday through a Looisville paper, wich wuz dropped off the cars at Secessionville, wich is the nearest station to us, and wich, I hapnin to be there, I picked up.

Ohio — 40,000 Ablishin !

Injeany — 20,000 Ablishin !

Pennsylvany — 20,000 Ablishin !

Iowa — 30,000 Ablishin !

ABLISHIN ! Wat a dreery waste uv Ablishin ! Not a single oasis uv Dimocrisy anywhere, — nary Aryrat on wich our ark kin rest in safety, — but all around us the mad waves uv Ablishnism rearin their crestid heads muchly.

AFTER THE FALL ELECTION.   Page 254.

I felt it my dooty to make this fact known to my neighbors; for, sposin that His Serene Highness' trip wood secure us enuff deestricts to make the next Congress safe, and consekently make us certin uv admission, they hed been makin arrangements for restorin things to their normal condishun, ez they were before the war.

In fact, two weeks before, in view of the expected success uv the Democracy, a meetin hed bin held on the subject. Some wuz for at once seezin the niggers wherever they cood be found, and puttin em at work; but the conservatives overruled this. They held that slavery hed bin abolished, and that it ought not be restored; in fact, that, to act in good faith, it cood not be reëstablished. Deekin Pogram announced a plan. The town authorities shood pass a ordinance for the proper government uv the niggers. Their good and ourn demanded it. For instance, they shood not be permitted to be out after 7 o'clock, P. M., in the evenin; they shoodent leave the plantashen onto wich they wuz employed; they shood work every day till 7; and to do away with the pernicious work uv the Freedmen's Bureau, no man and wife wich hed bin married by a chaplin uv the Bureau, or by any one else, shood be employed on the same plantashen, and also no father or mother

and child.   Sich ez violated these ordinances shood
be arrested by anybody, and fined ; and in default
uv payment uv the fine and costs, shood be sold to
the person who wood take his or her labor for the
shortest number uv years, and pay the fine and costs
aforesed.   " Ez a conservative," sed the Deekin, " I
sejest this plan."

" Do yoo want to know my definition uv the word
' conservative ? ' " sed Joe Bigler, a returned Confederate soljer, who, I bleeve, hez seen enough uv war.
" It's a man who goes a roundabout way to do a
devlish mean thing.   Deekin, why can't yoo go to
the devil by a straight road, ez I do ? "

The interupshen uv the demoralized wretch
wuzn't notist ; and ez the trustees uv the township wuz all present, the ordinance wuz passed,
and that night two thirds uv the niggers within
five miles uv the Corners wuz arrested and sold,
and within two weeks every one hed bin capcherd.

I hied me to the Corners, and the first man I saw
wuz Bascom, the grocery keeper, engaged in the
congenial biznis uv tappin a barrel uv contentment,
wich he hed just receeved.   I wuz a goin to tell him
the dread intelligence, when he caught site uv me.
" Taste that, Parson," sed he, holdin out a tin dipper

full. I drank it off, and one look at him onmand me. "Kin I o'ercloud that smilin cheek?" thot I, ez, in a fit uv absent-mindednis, — wich I hev every now and then, — I held out the empty dipper to be filled agin, wich it wuz. "No! for a time he shel be spared;" and I borrered his mule, and rode away pensively.

I wuz goin fust to Deekin Pogram's, for he wuz the most interested uv eny in the settlement. After the meetin mentioned above, the Deekin hed caused the arrest uv sich niggers ez he cood ketch, and had had em fined in sums uv $275 and uppards, wich bein unable, ez a rool, to pay the fine, he hed kindly bid em in.

He hed picked up, here and there, all uv his old servants, ceptin those wich hed bin killed in the army, and the few misguided ones wich hed made their way North, and that mornin the plantashen wuz to be reconstructed upon the old patriarkle system. Mrs. Deekin Pogram wuz marshellin four uv the likeliest wenches I ever saw in the kitchen; his son Tom wuz chuckin a yaller girl under the chin, wich hed bin born on the place about eighteen years before, and wich, owin to a unfortunate resemblance to the Deekin, hed caused a onpleasantnis between him and his wife, wich endid in the loss uv the most

17

uv his hair, and the sellin uv the girl's mother to
Noo Orleans.   The two girls hed each their waitin-
maids, and wuz a puttin them through their paces.
There hed bin some trouble in gittin em reconstructed, it bein deemed nessary to take the conseet out
uv em, wich they wuz all a doin.   Ez I rode up,
the old lady hed jest knocked one uv em down with
a fire-shovel, and wuz dancin a Highland fling onto
her prostrate body.   Almira, the oldest gal, hed her
fingers in the wool uv her gal; and tother one wuz
a thumpin hern to redose her to her proper level;
and the Deekin hisself wuz a deelin with one ongrateful wretch, who objected to bein put to work
on them terms, not realizin that the Bureau was
gone.   Ez the Deekin hed a revolver he yielded the
pint, and submitted to be flogged, wich the Deekin
wuz doin ez neatly ez I ever saw, considerin he hed
bin out uv practis four years.   He had him tied up
to a tree, and wuz a wollopin uv him gorjus.   While
he wuz a convinsin uv him with his whip that there
wuz trooth in the Skripter, and that Ham wuz reely
a servant unto his bretherin, I exclaimed, " Stop ! "
and immejitly whispered the appallin news in his
left ear (tother one hed bin chawed off in a misunderstandin at Bascom's the previous Sunday nite,
after servis).   Never shel I forgit the look uv woe

on that eminent Christian's face. The whip fell
from his nerveless hand; and with teers streemin
down his cheeks, washin up little streaks uv dirt in
the most heart-rendin manner, he gasped in a husky
voice to the wife uv his buzzum, "Cut him down,
Mirandy! The North's gone Ablishin, and the
d—d niggers will be free anyhow!" and the old
patriarch swooned away at my feet.

And sich an expression of anguish ez distorted
the face uv the Deekin's wife I hope never to see
agin. Droppin the shovel, she stood ez one petri-
fied, with her foot elevated in mid air, ez in the act
uv stompin, and uttering a shreek wich methinks I
hear ringing in my ears yet, she fell precisely ez she
stood, with her leg crooked ez ef 'twuz froze there.
Tom released the gal he wuz subdooin, and mountin
his horse rode off to the Corners without saying a
word; and unable to witness the distress uv that
stricken family, I made haste to mount my mule
and go to; while the niggers, feelin that they were
wunst more their own men and women, scattered in
every direction.

"Sich is the froots uv Radikelism," murmured I.
"Sich is the bitter cup fanaticism hez put to our
lips;" and castin one lingring look at the prostrate
forms uv the Deekin, his wife (with her foot insen-

sibly raised), and their two gushin daughters, I spurred the mule, and departed.

Wood that every Ablishnist in the North hed seen that site, and wuz possessed uv a sole to appreshate it! Then would they vote differently.

PETROLEUM V. NASBY, P. M.

(wich is Postmaster).

XXXVII.

*The October Elections. — Mr. Nasby's Opinion on
the Cause of the Defeat of the President.*

CONFEDRIT X ROADS
(wich is in the Stait uv Kentucky),
October 14, 1866.

I WUZ called in haste to Washington to be present at a Cabinet meetin called to consider the
causes uv the onparalleled loosenin uv the Nashnel
Union Johnson Dimekratic party in the various
States wich held elections on the 9th uv October
last. There wuz Seward, Wells, McCulloch, and
Randall present; but we missed Raymond and
Beecher, they hevin, I understand, played off onto us.

The President wuz gloomy. He hedn't anticipated
the defeat. He spected that, hevin showd hisself
through all the Northern States, ther ought to hev
ben enthoosiasm enough evolved to hev carried em
without trouble. The fault, he remarked, coodent
be with his policy. Ther wuz suthin so grand, so

sublimely simple in it, that it wuz incomprehensible to him why the people hedn't at once adopted it. "Why, look at it," sed he. "I offer the people uv the North peace, on the simple condishn uv sayin nothin more about the war, or the mutual trouble which they found theirselves into, and rushin into the arms uv their Southern brethren, and takin uv em back jist ez they went out. How, O! how cood they be so blind ez to refoose these olive branches?"

Randall replied that he coodent understand it; but he hed summoned a Postmaster to attend, wich he hed appinted on his solemn asshoorance that he cood carry enough Republicans over to our new party to defeat the Union member in that District, wich he notist by the papers wuz elected by a larger majority than he hed ever reseeved, and he wuz in waitin.

"Bring in the wretch!" shouted the President; and the guard brung him in. A mizable lookin objick he wuz. Ez soon ez he saw the stern eye uv the President fixed on him, he sunk to his knees, and lifted up his hands implorinly, without sayin a word.

"Speak!" sed the President. "Why the result in yoor Deestrict?"

"My liege," replied the wretched man, "I know

not. Faithfully I labored; but the people wood come into the house holdin their noses, and set a holdin uv em so long ez I wuz speekin, wich wuzn't conducive to displays of oratory. The papers wood publish my own utterances six months before, wich confused me somewhat; and the ablishnists would read at me yoor speeches, wich I coodent akkount for. I seekoored for yoo suthin like a dozen votes; but they wuz them ez stipulated for places under me, and I hed hard work to git em from the Union party, and they wuz sich ez did us more harm than good. And besides —— "

"Enuff!" sed Johnson. "Remove him."

And the poor fellow wuz bundled out.

Secretary Welles knowd wat wuz the matter. It come uv takin Grant and Farrygut along on the excursion. It distracted the attention uv the people. Hed there bin nobody but the President and the Cabinet along, there woodent hev bin nobody to hurrah for, and the sublime trooths, wich the President kin only jerk, wood hev impressed the people more than they did.

Seward wuz confident that the election wood hev bin all right cood it hev bin postponed ninety days; while McCullock attribooted it to the limited knowledge the masses hed uv Injeany bankin.

I wuz rekested to give my views, wich I did.

" My lords," sed I, " none uv you hev got the ijee. We wuz beet because we left the landmarks — that's wat ailed us, wuz the anshent landmarks. Wat hed we to go into this canvass with? Democrisy? Not any; for that wuz squelched at Philadelphia. Wat then? Why, the offises. Offises, in the abstract, is good. That little one which I hold in Kentucky I coodent be indoost to part with on no account; but yoo can't run a party on em, because there ain't enough uv em.

" My liege, on my return from the Philadelphia Convention I tarried a while in Berks county, which is in Pennsylvania, and is distinguished for the unanimity with which they vote Democracy. My liege, they learned down there mor'n six weeks ago that the war wuz over, and therefore yoo coodent stir em up on drafts. Taxes they had got used to, and that didn't move em ; and so the speaker wuz emptyin school-houses by talkin uv the results uv a glorious war, wich they all opposed, and praisin our mutual friend Seward, wich they had alluz hated as a Ablishnist, and hedn't heerd yet that he had jined the Demokracy. Wuz it any wonder that we went under? Ther ain't but one thing left to us, and that we strangely neglected. My liege, why wuz the

NIGGER not made the central figger this year, ez
before? They is the capital uv the Democrisy, its
refuge, its tower of strength. I spoke in Berks
county myself, following one of them new-fangled
Democrats, who hed set em all asleep talkin stuff
to em that they didn't understand. Mountin the
rostrum, I ejaculated, —

"'MEN AND BRETHREN, DO YOO WANT TO
MARRY A NIGGER?'

"'No! no!' they answered, straightenin up to-
wunst.

"'Do you want niggers for sons-in-law?'

"'No! no!'

"'Do you want laws to prevent you from marryin
niggers?'

"'Yes! yes!'

"'Do you want to be marched up to the polls by
those who tell you how to vote, beside a nigger?'

"'No! no!'

"'Then vote the Demekratic ticket.' And they
all replied, —

"'We will! we will!' and they did. You see,
your Exslency, the Demekratic mind isn't hefty
enough to comprehend them fine arguments ez to
constitootinality, et setry; and when a speaker deals
in em, they suspect his Dimocrisy, and fight shy uv

him. But nigger they kin all understand. It's soothin to the Dimekratic mind to be continyooally told that there is somebody lower down in the skale. They desire a inferior race, and therefore hev bin pullin the nigger down toward em for years. Did yoo not notis whenever we went it on the nigger we succeeded in awakenin an enthoosiasm, wich, when we neglected him, or selected other issues, we failed to get?

"It's based upon philosophical trooths. The poorer and meaner a man is, the more anxious he is to hev it understood that there's somebody still poorer and meaner than him. Hence, you notis, that them individooals who see a 5 cent peese so seldom ez to not know its nacher, and who keep the flag uv distress wavin from the seat uv their pants, — who, ef niggers wuz sellin at a cent a peese, coodent raise enough to buy the toe nail uv one, — is the most ardent friends of Slavery.

"That pitiful man wich jest left the presence wuz not to blame for the result in his Deestrick. He tried to earn his bread; but wat cood he do? The Ablishnists knowd he wuz bought with a price, and laffed at him. The Democrisy, sich ez voted, we'd hev got anyhow. Them ez didn't vote, nor do nothin, wuz the upper class, wich expected the offises themselves, and wuz disgusted accordinly.

"My liege, I hev spoke. Yoo can't do nothin with a new party; for yoo kin only git the Dimocrisy to jine it, and they won't do it onless the offises is throwd in. Yoo can't run the Dimocrisy on only one issue, and that's the nigger; for it's all they kin understand. So long ez the nigger exists, Dimocrisy endoors; when the race becomes extinct, the party dies. The two is indissolubly bound together; one wuz created for tother, and tother for one. When Noah cust Ham he laid the foundashens uv Dimocrisy. Ham wuz turned into a nigger because Noah got intoxicated. His misfortune originated with wine; and whisky, wich is the modern substitoot therefor, bein the motive power uv Dimocrisy, hez bin persekutin him ever sence. I attriboot the decline uv the Dimocrisy to the bleachin out uv the Afrikin, and that's why I oppose amalgamashen. Yoo can't hate a mulatter only half ez much ez yoo kin a full-blood; and it will be observed that the intensity uv Demokricy has decreased precisely in proportion to the scarcity uv pure blacks. Thus Demokrisy is committin suicide; it hez bin the means uv its own destruction.

"I don't know ez there's eny yoose uv talkin.

The Congressmen elected this fall continyoo in of-fis, my liege, jist precisely ez long ez yoo do, to a day, and by that time they'll hev it all fixed.   Noo York may change in our favor, but I think not. The break commenst in Maine, and it increased as it progressed.   We're gone in.   The Ablishnists laughs in glee, and the nigger shows all his ivories. We shel hold our places two years, and then farewell to our greatness.

"I pity yoo, my lord; but I can't help yoo.   Ez for myself, I kin save enuff out uv my Post Offis to start a small grocery at the expiration uv my term, and then farewell politics.   In that pleasant callin I'll flote down the stream uv Time, until Death closes the polls, and ends the struggle.   I hev sed."

The Conference ended with this : for they wuz all too much affected to say anything.   Seward mur-mered suthin about it would be all right in sixty days ; that there wuz no denyin that the people wuz happy ; but no one paid any attention to him.   I went home, leavin em all in tears.

PETROLEUM V. NASBY, P. M.

(wich is Postmaster).

XXXVIII.

" Will you have Andrew Johnson President or King?" — A Dream, in which Andrew Johnson figures as a King, surrounded by his Nobles.

CONFEDRIT X ROADS
(wich is in the Stait uv Kentucky),
October 24, 1866.

DREAMS is only vouchsafed to persons uv a imaginative and speritooal nacher, uv whom I am which. Ther aint anything gross or sensual about me that I know uv. Troo I eat pork, but that is to offset the effex uv whisky, wich, ef twasn't counteracted, wood make me entirely too etherial for this grovelin world. I eat pork, to restrain my exuberant imaginashun, and enable me to come down to the dry detail uv offish'l life — to fit me for the proper discharge uv my dooties ez a Postmaster. Whiskey lifts me above the posishun — pork brings me back agin. It's fat and greasy, like the pay and perquisites uv the Postmaster — it comes from the most nasty, senseless, and unclean uv animals, like our commishuns — in short, I recommend all uv Johnson's Postmasters to eat pork. It's ther nateral diet.

Last nite I partook uv a pound or so too much, and ez a consekence, didn't sleep well. While I wuz eatin (moistnin my lips with Looisville conslation the while), I wuz a musin onto Seward's question, whether they wood hev Johnson President or King, and while musin I fell in2 the arms uv Morfus. My mind bust loose from the body and sored. Ez I sunk to slumber, the narrow room, wich is at wunst my offis and dormitory, widened and enlarged, the humble chairs become suddenly upholstered in gorgus style, the taller dip become multiplied into thousands uv gorgus chandileers, the portraits uv His Highness the President, and the other Democrats on the wall, became alive. I comprehended the situation to wunst. ANDROO JOHNSON had cut the Gorjan knot with someboddy's sword, and hed carried out his Policy to its nateral concloosion. He was King, and wuz reignin under the title uv ANDROO THE I., and I wuz (in my dreem uv course) in his kingly halls.

It wuz, methawt, a reception nite. His High Mightiness wuz a sittin onto a elevated throne, covered with red velvet, and studded with diamonds,

and pearls, and onyxs, and other precious stones —
onto his head wuz a crown, and he wuz enveloped
into a robe uv black velvet, his nose and the balance
uv his face gleaming out like a flash uv litenin from
a thunder cloud. Lyin prostrate at the foot uv the
throne, doin the offis uv a footstool, wuz Charles
Sumner, wunst Senator, wich wuz typikle uv the
complete triumph we hed won over our enemies;
while doin other menial offices about the halls, wuz
Wade, Wilson, Fessenden, Sherman, and others who
hed opposed the change from a Republic to a King-
dom. They wuz clothed in a approprit costoom,
knee breeches and sich, and presented a pekoolyerly
imposin appearance.

Carriages containing the nobility began to arrive,
and ez they entered, the Grand High Lord Cham-
berlin uv the Palis, the Markis von Randall, an-
nounct em. " Dook de Davis ! " was ejackelatid, and
Jeffson entered. " Earl von Toombs," " Sir Joseph
E. Johnston," " Markis de Bouregard," " Count de
Pollard," and so forth.

Noticin that the titles I hed heerd wuz mostly
tacked to Southern men, I asked Giddy Welles, who
wuz standin by, why it wuz thus, and he sed that
Northners wuzn't reely fit for it. We wuz, he said,
a low, grovlin race, and coodent adapt ourselves to

the habits uv nobility. The South wuz shivelrus, and cood do it. They wuz given to tournaments and sich — they hed got accustomed to cirkus clothes, and cood wear a sword without its gettin awkwardly between the legs. Northern men, sich ez were faithful, wuz allowed to barsk in the smiles uv royalty, but it wuz in sich positions ez sooted their capacity. He, for instance, hed charge uv the royal poultry yard, a position which he bleved he filled to the entire satisfaction uv his beloved and royal master. He hed now four hens a settin, each on four eggs, and he hoped in the course uv two years, ef there wuz no adverse circumstances, to hev fresh eggs for the royal table. It wuz a position uv great responsibility, and one wich weighed upon him. Seward wuz privy counsler, Doolittle wuz steward uv the household, and Thurlow Weed wuz Keeper uv the King's revenue, and wuz a doin very well indeed.

By this time the company assembled. His Highness wuz in a merry mood, and unbendid hisself. Ther wuz a knot uv the nobility gathered in a corner, and after a earnest interview uv a minnit, Count Von Cowan advanced to the foot uv the throne, and on bendid knee demanded a boon.

" What, my faithful servitor, dost thou most desire? " sed His Highness.

" We wood, Your Majesty, hev the prisoners uv state brot into the presence, that we may make merry over 'em."

" It shel be done," sed His Majesty, and forthwith Baron von Steedman, who hed command uv the King's Household Body Guard, wuz sent for them. In a moment they wuz brot in. They wuz a mizable lookin set. Forney and Wendell Phillips wuz chained together, Fred Douglass and Anna Dickinson, Dick Yates and Gov. Morton, Ben Butler and Carl Shurz, Kelly and Covode, while Chase wuz tied to Horis Greely, onto whose back wuz a placard, inscribed, " The last uv the Tribunes ; " at wich Raymond, who left the Radikels and declared for the empire at precisely the rite time, and wuz now editor of the *Court Journal*, laffed immodritly. Some one exclaimed, " Bring in Thad Stevens ! " at wich His Majesty turned pale, and his knees smote together. " Don't, don't ! " sez he ; " he's strength enuff left to wag his tongue. Keep him away ! keep him away ! " and he showed ez much fear ez men do in delirum tremens when they see snakes.

Methawt I made inquiries, and found that things wuz workin satisfactory. Gen. Grant wuz in exile,

18

and Gen. Sheridan hed bin decapitatid for refoosin to acquiesce in the new arrangement. The country hed bin divided into dookdoms and earldoms, and sich, over wich the nobility rooled with undispooted authority. The principal men uv the North hed been capcherd and subdooed, and wuz a fillin menial positions in the palaces uv the nobility. No Lord or Dook or Earl considered himself well served onless he hed a half dozen Northern Congressmen in his house, while the higher grade uv nobility wuzn't content with anythin less than Guvners. The indebtednis uv the South to the North hed bin adjustid. A decree hed bin ishood to the effect that Northern merchants who shood press a claim agin a Southerner shood be beheaded and his goods confistikated. The question uv slavery hed bin settled forever, for the Dimekratic ijee uv one class to serve and one class to be served wuz fully establisht. There wuz now three classes uv society, the hereditary nobility, the untitled officials, and the people ; the latter, black and white, wuz all serfs, and all attached to the soil. Biznis wuz all done by foreigners, the policy uv the government bein to make the native born people purely agricultural peasantry. The nobility, desirin to make it easy for

em, giv em one sixth uv the produx uv the soil, re-
servin the balance for their own uses.

My dreem didn't continyoo long enuff for me to
ascertain whether I wuz a nobleman or not, but I
am uv the opinion that I wuz, for a servant, handin
me a pin to stick into Gen. Butler to make him roar
for the amoozement of the company, addressed me
ez " Yoor Grace," from wich I inferred that I wuz
one uv of the Lords spiritooal.   Unfortunitly at this
pint I awoke, and a sad awakenin it wuz.   The
gorjus halls hed vanished, the chandeleers hed vanished, the robes uv stait and jewels and sich wuz
gone, and I wuz in my offis, not " Yoor Grace,"
but merely a Postmaster in a Kentucky village!
Well, that is suthin.   Wat better is a nobleman?
He don't work, neither do I.   He drinks wine, it is
troo ; but I hev wat soots me better — whiskey fresh
from the still.   Yet my dreem may be realized, and
ef it is, I will endevoor to fill the position with
credit.   Who knows?

PETROLEUM V. NASBY, P. M.
(wich is Postmaster).

XXXIX.

A Cabinet Meeting. — Letters from Rev. Henry Ward Beecher, General Custar, Henry J. Raymond, and Hon. John Morrissey, each anxious to Preserve his Reputation. — A Sad Time at the White House.

CONFEDRIT ✕ ROADS
(wich is in the Stait uv Kentucky),
November 7, 1866.

I WUZ called to Washington by our patron Saint, the President, to comfort his wounded sperit. There ain't no disguisin the fact, — the sperit of Androo Johnson is wounded. He hez endoored the slings and arrers uv more outrajus fortune than any other man who hez lived sence the days uv Hamlick; more, indeed, than Hamlick endoored, twict over. Hamlick's father wuz pizoned, and his mother married agin afore her mournin clothes wuz wore out — suthin no savin, prudent woman would do; but what wuz that to wat A. JOHNSON endoors every day? Nothin.

The cabinet meetin to wich I wuz summoned wuz called for the purpose uv sheddin a tear or two over the election returns, and to consider a variety uv letters wich His Eggscellency hed receeved within a few days. I may remark that the cabinet hed a gloomy and mildewed look.

The fust wuz from Rev. Henry Ward Beecher. Mr. Beecher remarked that he had the highest possible respeck for the offis wunst held by the good Washinton, the great Adams, and the sainted Linkin. He omitted remarkin anythin about Peerce and Bookanan, out uv regard for the feelins uv the present incumbent, wich, ef he hed read History correct, wuz a ardent supporter uv the Administrashens uv both of them men, wich he considered stains upon the pages uv American history wich he cood wish mite be obliterated. But wat he desired to say wuz, that he hed a higher regard for the good opinion uv mankind in general than he hed for the good opinion uv the accidental incumbent uv any offis ; and ez he hed, in a hour uv temporary mental aberrashen, wich hed happily passed, endorsed the Administrashen, wich insanity hed worked evil unto him, he rekested, ez a simple act uv justice, that the President shood cause it to be known that he

(Beecher) wuz not considered by the Administrashen ez a supporter thereof.

"I do this," sed the writer, "becoz the impression
that I am in the confidence uv yoor Eggslency, wich
is onfortunately abroad, hez seriously DAMAGED MY
REPUTASHEN.

"Trooly yoors," et settry.

The readin uv this letter wuz follered by a minit
uv profound silence, wich wuz broken by the President.

"Let him pass," sed the great man who hez the
despensin uv the post offisis, "let him pass.   But
here is another," sed he, bustin into teers; "read
that."

It wuz from Gen. Custar, him uv the yaller hair,
wich hed some reputashen doorin the war ez a cav-
alry commander.   It wuz to the same effect.   He
hed, when he spozd that the policy uv the President,
wich he esteemed ez he must any man who held the
exalted position wunst okkepied by the good Washinton, the great Jefferson, and the sainted Linkin ——

"The ongrateful dog doesn't respect ME!" sed
Androo; "it's the offis I fill;" and he bust into
a fresh flood.

—— When he spozed the President's policy wuz sich ez a soljer and patriot cood endorse, he endorsed it. But he diskivered that it led him, back foremost, into company wich, doorin the late war, he hed alluz visited face foremost and on hossback ; and therefore, to SAVE HIS REPUTASHUN, he must beg that the President wood give it out that he (Gen. Custar) wuz not, nor never hed bin, a supporter uv his policy, and oblige

Yoors trooly, ez before.

I wuz too hart-broken at this to make any reply, and Cowan and Doolittle wuz in the same fix. The Kernelcy wich wuz given to Custar to keep him in posishen hed bin promised to a Demokratic captin, who wuz led by a company in the first Bull Run fight, and who threw up in disgust the next day, not likin the manner in wich the war wuz bein conducted ; but now the Kernelcy wuz gone, and Custar too ; and wat wuz worse, there wuz no sich thing to be thot uv ez dismissin him. The entire company yoonited in minglin their teers.

The next letter wuz read by Seward, ez it wuz addressed to him. It wuz from Raymond. He opened with the remark that for the Presidential office he hed the highest respeck. Aside from the considerashen that it hed bin wunst okkepied by the good Washinton, the great Adams, and the sainted Linkin, the President mite be considered the Father of his country, hevin so large a number of helpless children to provide for; and besides, he hed a instinctive respeck for the dispenser of anything. It wuz difficult for him, bein a open and simple-minded man, not to adhere to the President; but ——

"Good Heavens!" shreeked Johnson, "that little fox ain't a goin to speak uv HIS reputashen!"

"Dooty requires the reedin uv the entire dockeyment, painful to my feelins ez it may be," sed Seward. "He concloods thusly: —

"'I am forced to ask yoo, ez one enjoyin confidenshel relations with Him who occupies the Presidenshel chair, to hev it given out that I stand in opposition to him. A doo REGARD FOR MY REPUTASHEN impels me to this course. I remain

"'Yoors Trooly.'"

There wuz 2 or three more. Gen. Carey uv Ohio, requested the President to remove him from his Collectorship, ez the holdin uv it wuz INJOORIN HIS REPUTASHEN. A editor out West, who wuz sedooced into takin a Post Offis, begged to hev it taken off his hands, that he might save his circulashen before it wuz everlastinly too late. And finally we come to wun, the seal uv wich wuz a coat-uv-arms — bull dog rampant, bowie-knife couchant, supported by trottin horses, on a field uv green cloth. It wuz from Hon. John Morrisey, who hed jest ben elected to Congress in Noo York.

Mr. Morrisey remarked that, ez one uv the pillars uv the Democrasy, he felt he hed a rite to speek. He wished it to be understood that he washed his hands uv any connection with Johnson or his party. He hed seed a lite. In States where the Democrasy, uv wich he wuz a piller, hed tied themselves to Johnson, they hed gone down to a prematoor grave. Respeck for the high offis restrained him from sayin that the Democrasy coodent carry sich a cussid load ; but he wood say that the result uv the election in Noo York, where they dependid solely on muscle and nigger, wich is the reel Democratic capital, and succeeded, while where the Democrasy wuz loaded down with Johnsonianism, they failed, satisfied him that the President wuz a inkubus. He sed this with all doo respeck for the offis. Mr. Morrisey further remarked that he hed also personel reasons for makin this request. He commenced in a humble position, and hed filled the public eye long enuff to satisfy his modist ambishen. He hed walloped Sul-

livan and Heenan ; he hed owned the fastest horses,
and won more money at faro than any man in
Amerika.   His ambishen wuz satisfied, so fur ez he
wuz concerned ; but he hoped to leave behind him,
for his infant son (wich wuz only twelve years uv
age, and wich hed a development uv intelleck and
muscle remarkable for one so tender, havin already
walloped every boy in the skool to wich he wuz a
goin), he desired to leave that son a honorable
name.   It hed bin given out that he wuz a supporter uv the individooal who okkepied the Presidenshel offis, and it wuz injoorin him.   He wished
that stigma removed.   A REGARD FOR HIS REPU-
TASHEN forced him to insist upon it.

And this epistle wuz dooly signed,

his

JOHN ✕ MORRISSEY, M. C.

mark.

There wuz silence in the Cabinet.   This last
stroke intensified the gloom wich hed settled onto
the Government; and ez I turned my tear-be-
dewed eyes, I saw the great drops coursin down
the cheeks uv every one present.   Mr. Seward retired without sayin anythin about ninety days, and
one by one they all departed.

It wuz a solemn time.   There wuz other letters

yet to be read, but no one hed the heart to open em.
I made a move in that direckshun, but Androo prevented me. " I'm sick," murmured he, in a husky
voice, which showed that his hart wuz peerced.
" Help me to bed." I saw the great man bury his
intellectool head beneath the snowy kivrin uv his
oneasy couch, all but the nose, which in him is the
thermometer uv the sole, and which accordinly
glowed, not with the yoosooal brilliant hue, but
with a dull, dead, and ghastly bloo. Noticin the
convulsive heavins uv the kivers, which betrayed
the agitashen uv the breast beneath, I whispered in
his ear, ez I handed him his nite drink uv rye whisky flavored with bourbon, that· he hed one hold, ez
Delaware hed sustained him. A flush uv satisfaction passed over his nose, but it subsided in an in-
stant. " Troo," gasped he, " it's ourn now ; but
before the next election a couple uv them Massachoosits ablishnists will buy the cussid State, and
re-people it to soot em ; " and he gave a convulsive
gasp, and sank into a troubled slumber.

It wuz a tetchin occasion.

PETROLEUM V. NASBY, P. M.

(wich is Postmaster).

XL.

A Sermon upon the November Elections, from the Text, "No man putteth New Wine into Old Bottles," with a Digression or Two.

CONFEDRIT X ROADS
(wich is in the Stait uv Kentucky),
November 16, 1866.

WHEN the news uv the result of the Illinoy election reached the Corners, there wuz a feelin uv oneasiness wich was trooly affectin; but when the crushin intelligence arove that Hoffman wuz beeten in Noo York, there wuz a prostration wich wuz only ekalled when the intelligence of Lee's surrender reached us. We expected defeat in Illinoy, and some uv the other States, but we hed hopes that Noo York wood go Dimocratic, that His Eggslency mite hev some show uv backin by the people, and consekently some excoose for continyooin to enforce his policy. But that hope wuz taken from us, and uv the entire populashen, I wuz the only one who hed suffishent stamina to preserve the semblance uv cheerfulness, and that wuz only on akkount uv my hevin the Post Offis. Elections can't take that from me: it is a rock wich the waves uv popler indignashen can't wash away, thank the Lord! for ef they cood, how many uv us wood to-day be holdin our places? Still, I felt overwhelmed, and sorrowfully I entered Bascom's. There, with their heads bowed in sorrer, and tears flowin from their venrable eyes, sot Deekin Pogram, Elder Slathers, and a few others uv the Saints, who, ez I entered, mekanikally rose, and stood afore the bar; mekanikally Bascom, who wuz likewise bowed down with greef, sot out the invigorator; mekanikally we dosed ourselves, and still in a daze, mekanikally I moved out without payin, Bascom bein too full uv sorrer to notis it.

It wuz deemed proper, in view uv the great calamity, that services shood be held in the church, and at 2 P. M., wich with us mite be sed to mean post mortem, we slowly and sadly filed in, the only smilin countenance in site bein that uv a nigger at the door, who wuz to-wunst beltid over the head for lookin happy.

I gave out the hymn, —

"Broad is the road wich leeds to death," —

and it wuz sung with tetchin pathos. After the
weepin hed subsided, and I got my feelings calmed
down so ez to permit me to speek, I commenst
explainin to em the causes uv the result. It wuz, I
sed, a chastenin sent onto us for our sins; a stripin
becoz we hed exalted our horn in our pride; that,
gloryin in the possession uv the post offices, the
collectorships, the assessorships, and sich, we hed
become vain-glorious and puffed up, and careless in
performance uv dooties. Ther wuz niggers in Kentucky a goin about free, and impiously settin at
naught the decrees uv Providence, wich condemned
em to be servants uv their brethren; and heer I
digressed to eloocydate a pint. I hed seen stricters
in a Boston paper onto the common practice uv
amalgamashen in the South, wich paper held up
the practis to the condemnashen uv pious men.
"My brethren," sed I, "them Boston Ablishnists
hev no cleer understandin uv the Skripter. When
Ham wuz cust by Noar, wat wuz that cuss? '*He
shel be a servant unto his brethren.*' Not unto
strangers; not unto the Philistine, or the Girgeshite,
or the Millerite, but unto his brethren! How cood
he be servant unto his brethren except thro amalgamashen? Onless we amalgamated with em, how
wood the male niggers be our brethren? O, my

brethren! we wuz obliged to do these things, that the Skripters mite be fulfilled; and to the credit uv the Southern people, be it sed, that they never shrunk from the performance uv dooty. The per cent. uv yeller niggers in this State attests how faithful Kentucky hez bin."

But to resoom. We hev sinned in permittin skools to come in, and unfit um for their normal and skriptural condishen; but these is not all. My brethren, go to Esq. McGavitt's, and get the township Bible, and search till yoo find this yer tex: —

"And no man puttith new wine into old bottles, else the new wine doth bust the bottles, and the wine is spilled."

My brethren, wich is the bottles? The Dimocrisey, uv course; and the most uv em may be considered old ones. We hev actid as bottles, carrying about flooids — not percisely wine, but the modern substitoot therefor — from our earliest infancy. Wich is new wine? The Ablishnists wich follered Johnson, uv course. New wine is frothy; so wuz they. New wine fizzes; so did they. New wine hez strength for a minnit; so hed they. New wine is unreliable; so wuz they. At Philadelphy the puttin uv this new wine into old bottles wuz accomplished; at that accursed place anshent Dimocrisy,

wich beleeves in Ham and Hagar, met and fell onto
the nex uv Seward and Doolittle, wich invented
Ablishinism, and we mingled our teers together;
the new wine wuz put into the venerable old bottle
uv Dimocrisy, and notwithstandin we hooped it
with Federal patronage, it busted, and great wuz
the bust thereof; and the fragments uv the bottles
wuz prone onto the earth, and the new wine is
runnin round permiscus. So wuz the Skripter
fulfilled.

And, my brethren, while yoo are at the Squire's
huntin up that tex, keep on till yoo find another, to
wit : —

"No man also seweth a piece uv old cloth onto a new garment, else the new piece that filleth it up taketh it away from
the old, and the rent is made worse."

My hearers, Democrisy went to Philadelphy in a
soot uv gray, wich it hed bin a wearin for five
years. It wuz trooly old, and ther wuz greevious
rents in it, made mostly by bayonets, and sich. O,
why wuzn't we content to wear it? Why wuz we
not satisfied with it? Agin wuz the Skripters fulfilled. We patched up the Confedrit gray with
Federal blue; we put onto the back, Seward; onto
the knees, Randall; onto the shoulders, Cowan;
and onto the seat, Johnson, and they wuz stitched

together with Post Offisis. But it didn't hold. The
Skripters wuz fulfilled; the old cloth wuz rotten,
and one by one patches fell off, somewhat dirtied,
and takin with em a part uv the old, and the rents
is bigger than before. Our coat is busted at the
elbows, our pants is frayed round the bottoms, out
at the knees, and from behind the flag uv distress
waveth drearily in the cold wind.

My brethren, we will succeed when we stick to
our integrity. Wat wuz the yoose uv our assoomin
what we did not hev? Wat wuz the sence uv our
askin our people to vote for Kernels for Congris
wich hed, doorin the war, drafted their sons? Wat
wuz the yoose uv talking Constooshnel Amend-
ments to men who spozed that Internal Improve-
ments and a Nashnel Bank wuz still the ishoo?
Wat wuz the yoose uv lettin go our holt on nigger
equality, wich is the right bower, left bower, and
ace uv the Democrisy, — its tower uv strength, its
anker and cheefest trust, and wich is easy uv com-
prehension, and eminently adapted to the Democratic
intelleck, — and takin up questions wich will all
be settled ten years afore they begin to comprehend
em? In breef, wat wuz the sense, my brethren, in
puttin new wine into old bottles? — uv patchin old
cloth with new? Let us be warned, and never
repeet the fatle error.

19

The congregashen dispersed somewhat sadly, but ez they gathered at Bascom's to discuss the sermon, I wuz gratified at observin a visible improvement in their temper. Bascom hisself bussled around lively; Deekin Pogram remarked that probably it wuz unskriptooral to put new wine into old tubs, but ez he didn't hev an ijee that the prohibishen extendid to new whisky, he'd resk it, bust or no bust, and he pizened hisself very much in the old style, and Elder Slather and Kernel McPelter so far recovered their sperits ez to hang the nigger I menshend in the beginnin ez lookin pleased at the church. The Corners is rapidly gettin itself agin.

PETROLEUM V. NASBY, P. M.

(wich is Postmaster).

XLI.

A Few Last Words. — The Writer hereof bids his Readers Farewell, and hurls a Trifle of Exhortation after them.

CONFEDRIT X ROADS
(wich is in the Stait uv Kentucky),
November 19, 1866.

POETS hev remarked a great many times, too tejus to enoomerate, that " farewell " is the saddistist word to pronounce wich hez to be pronounst. It may be so among poets, wich are spozd to be a continyooally carryin about with em a load uv sadnis, and sensibilities, and sich; but I hev never found it so. The fact is, it depends very much on how yoo say it, under wat circumstances, and to whom. Wen, in my infancy, I wuz inkarseratid in the common jail uv my native village, in Noo Gersey, a victim to the prejudisis uv twelve men, who believed, on the unsupportid testimony uv three men, and the mere accident uv the missin property bein found in my possession (notwith-

standin the fact that I solemnly asshoored em that I
didn't know nothin about it, and if I did it, it must
hev bin in a somnamboolic state), that I hed bin
guilty uv bustin open a grosery store, and takin
twelve boxes uv cheroot cigars, I asshoor yoo that,
at the end uv the sentence, — hevin bin fed on bread
and water, — the sayin of farewell to the inhuman
jailer wuzn't at all onpleasant.   Likewise, when, in
the State uv Pennsylvany, in the eggscitin campane
uv 1856, I votid twict or four times for that eminent
and   gilelis   patriot,   Jeems   Bookannon,   and   wuz
hauled up therefor, and sentenced by a Ablishn
Judge to a year in the Western Penitentiary, after
an elokent speech, in wich I reviewed the whole
question at issue between the parties, and ashoored
him that my triflin irregularity in the matter uv
votin grew out uv an overweenin desire for the sal-
vashen uv my beloved country, — that, feelin that
rooin wuz ahead uv us, onless that leveler Fremont
wuz defeated, I felt that my conshence wood not be
easy onless I did all in my power to avert the evil,
— when I emerged from them gloomy walls, with
one soot uv close, and a tolable knowledge uv the
shoemakin biznis, wuz it a sad thing for me to say
" Farewell " to the grim jailer, whose key turned

one way wuz liberty, and tother way captivity?
Nary.

These two instances, I beleeve, is the only ones in
wich I hev ever hed to say farewell. In the course
uv my long and checkered career (I do not here
allood to the style uv clothin in the Penitentiary), I
am, when I think uv it, surprised at the compar-
atively few times wich I ever left a place at wich I
hed bin stayin, in daylite! I ginerally went in the
nite, —

> "Foldin my tent like the Arab,
> And ez silently steelin away,"

hevin too much sensibility to be an onwillin witnis
uv the agony uv landladies, when they diskivered
that I cood not pay. Knowin the softnis uv my
heart, I hev alluz hed a great regard for my feelins.

Still, I feel some disinclinashen to commence
sayin Farewell at this time. I wood like to continyoo this work. Methinks I wood like to go on
pilin up pages ontil the Dimocrisy uv the Yoonited
States wuz thoroughly indoctrinatid with *my* Dimocrisy. But it is impossible.

I bid my readers farewell in a period uv gloom
rarely ekalled, and never surpast, for the Democrisy.
Never in my recollekshun wuz the party in sich a
state uv abject cussitood. The Northern States hev

slipt from our grasp one by one, ontil none remains wich we kin fondly call ourn. The Border States are losin their Dimocrisy, and rallyin under the black banner uv Ablishinism; and the ten States which we kin control onfortinitly ain't got no voice in the Guvment. From the mountin tops uv Maine, and the level pararies uv Illinoy, the remnants uv the Dimocrisy holler to us uv the South, "Be firm! we'll stand by yoo!" and from the rich cotton fields uv the South the Dimocrisy holler to them uv the North, "Keep up yoor sperits! we are troo to yoo!" all uv wich is very cheerin, when them uv the North is in sich a hopelis minority ez to be unable to elect a township constable, and them in the South hain't got no vote at all!

I appeal, however, with the rest uv the leaders, to the Dimocrisy to remain firm. Suthin will come in time, — what, I can't, with any degree uv certinty, now state; but suthin will come. The Ablishnists cannot alluz rool. The cuss uv the old Whig party wuz, that the respective individooal members thereof cood read and write, and hed a knack uv doin their own thinkin, and therefore it cood not be brot into that state uv dissipline so nessary to success ez a party. That same cuss is a hangin onto the Ablishnists. They hung together from 1856 to 1860

coz there wuz wat they called a prinsipple at stake ;
and on that prinsipple they elected Linkin. They
wood hev fallen to peeces then, but our Southern
brethren decided to commence operashens for the
new goverment it hed so long desired; and the
overwhelmin pressur uv the war smothered all miner
ishoos and all individooal feelin, and they hung together long enough to see that throo. Now, still
for the principle wich welded em doorin the war,
they are holdin together yit, and probably will ontil
they think this question wich they are disposin of is
disposed of. Then they will split up, and our openin
is made. We hev a solid phalanx, wich they can't
win over or detach from us. We hev them old veterans who voted for Jaxon, and who are still votin
for him. We hev them sturdy old yeomanry who
still swear that Bloo Lite Fedralism ought to be put
down, and can't be tolerated in a Republikin Goverment, and who, bless their old souls! don't know
no more what Bloo Lite Fedralism wuz than an
unborn baby does uv Guy Fawkes. We hev that
solid army uv voters whose knees yawn hidjusly,
and whose coats is out at elbows, and whose children go barefoot in winter, while their dads is a
drinkin cheap whiskey, and damin the Goverment
for imposin a income tax. We hev the patriotic

citizins whose noses blossom like the lobster, and who live in mortal fear uv nigger ekality ; and we hev John Morrissey's constitooents.

These classes argyment won't move, and reasonin won't faze.   They like to abooze the Goverment for levyin taxes, hopin to deseeve somebody into the idea that they pay taxes, and that it bears hard onto em ; and they oppose nigger ekality becoz it soothes em, lik laudnum, to think that there is somebody in the country lower down than themselves.   The Dimocrisy alluz hed these, and alluz will.

Ez I remarked, the Ablishnists, when releeved uv the pressure now bearin onto em, will grow fractious, and split, and these classes will hev no trouble to git into a majority, and then our time comes.

The discouraged Dimokrat may say that preech-ers, and noosepapers, and Sundy skools, and sich, are underminin their party.   In time they will, but not yet.   There is still whisky in the land, and the nigger is not yet extinct.   Uv wat danger is preech-ers to these men, when yoo coodent git one uv em within gun-shot uv one? and wat harm is noose-papers to em, when they can't read?   Besides, we are not at the end uv our resources yet.   When the wust comes to the wust, there is the nigger left us. When he is no longer uv use to us ez he is now, —

when the prejoodis is so far removed ez to invest
him with the suffrage, — then WE'LL give him the
ballot, — WE'LL lead him up out uv Egypt, and we'll
make him vote with us. The Dimocrisy never yet
failed to control all uv the lower orders uv sosiety.
They hev the lowest grade uv the furriners; they
hev Delaware and Maryland; they hev Noo York
city and Suthern Illinoy; and ef the nigger gets the
ballot afore he does the spellin-book, he's ourn beyond peradvencher.

Again: Ef our politikel stumiks isn't yet toned
up to swallerin the nigger, we kin compermise on
the Mexican. That country Johnson hez his eagle
eye on now, and ef we demand it, he'll take it.
Wat a glorious prospeck opens to us! Mexico
wood cut up into at least twenty States, wich, added
to the ten we hev, wood make a clean majority wich
we cood hold for years. Massachoosets cood do
nuthin in Mexico. The Greasers ain't adapted to
Massachoosets. Ef they sent their long-haired teachers there with their spellin books, they'd end their
labors by lettin a knife into their intestines for the
clothes they wore, wich wood put a check on the
mishnary biznis. They are, it is troo, several de-
grees lower in the skale uv humanity than the niggers, but then they ain't niggers, and we cood marry

em without feelin that we'd degraded ourselves. Ther is undoubtedly cusses on em, but the only cuss we hev Constooshnel objections to is the cuss uv Ham, and that they ain't labrin under. Mexico affords us room for hope ; we never shel run out uv material for Dimocratic votes until she is convertid, and but few mishnaries wood hev the nerve to tackle her.

Therfore I say to the Dimocrisy, be uv good cheer ! Ther's a brite day a dawnin. We hev now the Post Offisis, and nothin short uv an impeach-ment kin take em from us for two years. We may be beaten in 1868 ; it may be that our managin men promised the nominashen to our present Head — A. JOHNSON ; but I hope not. Ef we are laid out agin, we kin console ourselves with the reflection that we're yoost to it, and we kin go on hopin for the good time that must come.

Let us hold onto our faith, and continyoo to run, hopin eventooally to be glorified. Let us remember that all the majorities agin us don't change the fact that Noah cust Ham, and that Hagar wuz sent back to her mistress. Let us remember that Paul, or some one uv them possels, remarked, " Servance, obey yoor masters," and that, under Ablishn rool, we are exposed to the danger uv marryin niggers.

Let us still cherish the faith that evenchooally, when reason returns, the Amerikin people will not throw away the boon we offer em uv fillin the cuss uv labor imposed by the Almity for disobedience in the garden, ez the Dimocrisy served in the army, by substitoot, and persevere even unto the perfeck end. When this good time is come, then will the anshent Dimocrisy, uv wich I hev bin to-wunst a piller and a ornament for thirty years, triumph, and the position wich I now hold, wich is rather too temporary to be agreeable, be continyood unto me for keeps, and layin off the armor uv actooal warfare, I shel rest in that haven uv worn-out patriots, — a perpetooal Post Offis. May the day be hastened! Farewell!

Petroleum V. Nasby, P. M.
(wich is Postmaster).

The End.